FAMOUS MAGICIANS IN HISTORY

A HISTORY OF MODERN MAGIC

SAM FURY

WARNINGS AND DISCLAIMERS

The information in this publication is made public for reference only.

Neither the author, publisher, nor anyone else involved in the production of this publication is responsible for how the reader uses the information or the result of his/her actions.

CONTENTS

THANKS FOR YOUR PURCHASE

Did you know you can get FREE chapters of any SF Nonfiction Book you want?

https://www.SFNonfictionBooks.com/Free-Chapters

You will also be among the first to know of FREE review copies, discount offers, bonus content, and more.

Go to:

https://www.SFNonfictionBooks.com/Free-Chapters

Thanks again for your support.

INTRODUCTION

Sit for a moment and close your eyes: think back to your childhood, when simple magic tricks entertained you for years. When going to the circus or seeing magic tricks performed filled you with absolute joy.

Think back to the first time you encountered a magic trick, whether it was your grandfather pulling a coin from behind your ear or a birthday party where a friend had a magician who made a rabbit appear from his hat.

We all have amazing memories like these when it comes to magic. The sense of wonder and mystery it filled us with was spectacular beyond belief.

It created a sense of wonder and curiosity in all of us, allowing us to believe that anything in the universe could happen. We could do and become whatever we wanted, even someone who did magic tricks.

As we grew older though, we slowly started to realize that while there was some substance to what these performers did, it was something far more mundane than some magical force from outside our scope of view that allowed these tricks to happen. We grew up and our understanding that it was merely trickery and illusion that created these wonderful scenes set in.

Take a journey through the decades and see what inspired so many magicians. This book will cover the important background surrounding all the prominent magicians who influenced modern day magic, as well as the tricks and stunts they did to make them famous.

Beyond the background, this book will impart information on the influence the earlier magicians had on modern day magic, and how modern day magic can be found in our everyday lives. The hope is that you delve deep into this outlook on modern magic and its predecessors and learn what it truly means to be a magician, and how wonderful the tricks and magic are that you have learned in the previous two books.

May your reading journey be magical!

WHAT IS MAGIC?

And above all, watch with glittering eyes the whole world around you because the greatest secrets are always hidden in the most unlikely places. Those who don't believe in magic will never find it. — Roald Dahl

Magic is something that is defined differently by everyone. One person may think that it is magical when butterflies appear out of nowhere, while someone else will argue that it is the way your eyes are focused on a magician's hands when he does a disappearing trick. It is the wonder and mystery that makes magic the spontaneous and amazing thing that it is.

The word *magic* stems from the Greek word *mageia*. This came to play because Persian priests who were known as *magosh* would come to pray during the Persian and Greek war. This term was slowly adopted to represent the rituals that Persian priests would do during the war, and later came to be known as anything that was considered foreign or unorthodox to the Greeks.

Slowly but surely, the occurrence of illusionary tricks became more common and any sort of entertainment that was part of illusions was categorized as 'magic,' and any sort of entertainment surrounding illusions or effects of illusions came to be known as 'magic tricks.'

Magic can be split into different groups and collections: mainly illusionary magic, stage magic, coin magic, and card magic. The latter two fall into a category called 'close-up magic.' There are also those who believe in unnatural magic, mainly connected to the occult and witchcraft, which of course is very far removed from the type of modern magic one finds today. Magic can be described as one of the oldest arts and entertainment methods in the world.

Timeline

In this section, the basics of what magic is and where it came from will be covered. It is important to know the stepping stones that were taken to get us to where we are now. Magic was not always pulling white rabbits from top hats and sawing pretty ladies in half. In fact, most of the early magic that can be found stems from disappearing acts.

The first recorded magic act was in 2700 B.C. in Egypt. While there is no certain evidence of this, as the wall painting gives no sure context of the magician who did the trick, it is believed that Dedi was the first known magician who used cups and balls as a form of entertainment.

Slowly but surely magic grew and the most common place magic could be found was in Greece. Various ancient Greek myths often refer to the cups-and-balls conjuring trick. More interesting was the way that nymphs and divination origin was prominent in Greek mythology, and how women in these times were linked to most magical encounters, whether with necromancy or magic. It is important to note that during this time necromancy was far more focused on dealing with the dead, and making sure they were at peace, whereas magic was used for other reasons, such as making sure women could bear male sons, so in many ways, 'magic' was more associated with sorcery or witchcraft.

During the Dark Ages magic grew even more prominent, but not for the reasons that we follow today. 'Dark magic' was at the helm, carrying connections believed to be part of the occult rather than entertainment purposes. The connection to the occult and the mystery behind it motivated others to do more research, spending time on debunking the occult, and in turn it only helped magic in entertainment grow stronger in modern times.

The Middle Ages were no different for magic; in fact, some may say it was even worse. Magic was seen as part of the occult and witch-craft. This only fueled circus and street performers to stick to normal and rather basic trickery, such as cups and balls and sleight of hand. This is where the trade of cheating by using sleight 0f hand has been believed to originate.

Since not a lot is known about magic and trickery up until the Middle Ages, not a lot of information can be thoroughly present, but from the 1500s onward there is more documentation and publications that can be found and studied with regards to the magic we know and love these days.

The first book that was published on Magic was titled *Discoverie of Witchcraft*. This book, published by Reginald Scot in 1584, was dedicated to the occult, but also spoke about how *magic* was linked to the occult. The book's main goal of course was to stop the persecution of those who dabbled in trickery, but by the 17th century thousands of Scot's books had been burned, perhaps out of fear more than anything else.

The publication did not stop there though. In 1634, *Hocus Pocus Junior: The Anatomie of Legerdemain* was published. This book was one of the very first that included how to perform the cups-and-balls trick. It is interesting to note that 12 different editions of this book were printed and published.

Isaac Fawkes, one of the most prominent magicians in English history, retired in 1720. He had various tricks and magic in his repertoire, including the 'bag of many eggs' and the trick of the card on the ceiling. William Hogarth had a painting called 'Bartholomew Fair', where Fawkes' booth was featured, here it is called 'Dexterity of Hands.' As part of Fawkes' shows, he also included contortionists, as well as various impressionists.

One of the main figures in the 18th century magic era was Joseph Pinetti, who was commonly known as the first magician whose performance of the thumb-tie effect was recorded. The thumb-tie effect can be seen as a matter through matter effect. During the trick, one's thumbs are crossed over and then tied together using a piece of rope, but by adding slack to the rope, one can assure that even if the rope is tied extremely tightly, that you will always be able to escape.

The year 1805 marked one of the most important years for magic as a whole. This specific year marked the birth of Jean Eugène Robert-Houdin. He is considered to be the father of modern magic, as he was one of the first magicians to move his craft from street and circus performances to large stages and drawing rooms.

Next, 1874 marked the birth of one of the most common known magicians in the world: Harry Houdini. Harry Houdini was well known for his amazing escape tricks. His real name, Ehrich Weiss, was not commonly known and he was more commonly known as the 'King of Handcuffs.'

Publication changes towards magic and how it was portrayed towards the public came in 1876, when Professor Louis Hoffman (Angelo John Lewis) published *Modern Magic,* which explained the method behind tricks and magic and the different apparatus used by magicians.

The year 1877 marked the first opening of a magic store, known as Martinka and Co. The store is still in existence after all these years. Owners Francis and Antonio Martinka employed Houdini here in 1919.

The only known man to oppose Houdini was born in 1894, named Dai Vernon, or The Man who Fooled Houdini. He is known as one of the most influential 20th century magicians to date. Dai Vernon was one of the few magicians in the early 1900s who competed against Houdini as a performer and could successfully do so.

Lewis Davenport Ltd. was established and founded in 1898. Like Martinka and Co., it is also one of the oldest family magic businesses to date that is still in existence.

The year 1902 was when one of the most important books on cards and card magic was written and published. *Expert at the Card Table* was written by S. W. Erdnase and published by The Charles T.

Powner company. To this date, it is one of the most important publications for card magicians.

The year also marked the establishment and founding of the Society of American Magicians at Martinka's. It is one of the biggest magical societies in the world that still exists to this day.

Three years later, in 1905 The Magic Circle was formed. This is one of the more stricter societies, having expelled many of their presidents for allegedly exposing the society. The South African Magical Society was formed in 1918 and has been rumored to be closely affiliated with the London Magic Circle. The Australian Society of Magicians, considered to be the fouth oldest of the magic societies in the world, was founded in 1907 in Sydney.

The most important and influential books, when it comes to magic and the theory behind it, was published in 1911 by authors Nevil Maskelyne and David Devant, and is aptly titled *Our Magic*.

Houdini's first performance of the vanishing elephant was captured in 1918 on January 7th at the Hippodrome in New York City. His untimely demise in 1926 resulted in a wonderful statuary bust of him at his grave, one of the only of its kind in the Jewish cemetery.

The finger chopper, one of the most common tricks for new magicians to learn, was invented by Edward M. Massey in the 1940s.

Various publications, considered to be the important first steps for each category, have been published. Books like *Royal Road to Card Magic* written by Jean Hugard and Fred Braue are among the most fundamental for those wanting to dabble in card magic, and the book *Modern Coin Magic*, written by J. B. Bobo has been considered the holy grail in text when it comes to coin magic.

Another well known name, David Copperfield, was born in 1956. He has revolutionized magic as it stands today. Four years later, Lance Burton was born in Louisville, Kentucky.

The year 1963 marks the wonderful start of The Magic Castle. Bill, Milt, and Irene Larson converted a 1908 mansion into a center for magic, which led to more similar establishments, and in 1972 The Magic Towne House was opened. Ed Davis was the founding father but Dorothy Dietrich and Dick Brookz took over after a few years. Various of the greats have performed at the Magic Towne House in New York, including Rocco Silano, Jeff McBride, Frank Garcia, and Eric DeCamps.

Dorothy Dietrich's greatness does not stop there, and she became one of the first and to date, the only woman in history to attempt and successfully pull off the bullet-catch-in-her-mouth trick. It was done in a controlled environment, but due to the international press it received, the trick has been dubbed as one of the stunts that even Houdini had feared in his life.

The Houdini Museum that opened in Scranton in 1988 moved the entire exhibit from the Magic Towne House and became the first and original museum when it comes to anything and everything Houdini.

The year 1994 marks the revolutionization of magic, as the first world wide web magic store opened. This meant that the way that magic could be taught and distributed changed the entire magic-learning process.

Three years later, another big name in the magic world started bringing street magic to America. David Blaine played a revolutionary role in how street magic has been perceived and used.

Criss Angel had his first show in 1998 at the Madison Square Garden in New York City, and this prompted a second show, called *Mindfreak*, that continued to run until 2003. Magic kind of slowed somewhat between the early 2000s and where it is today. A lot of magicians are using social media as a way to get themselves out there, compared to doing large-scale shows at event halls.

Dynamo started his social media career and in 2011 he became internationally known when his series *Dynamo:Magician Impossible* was released. The popularity of the show continued on, rewarding him with two more seasons.

The hundreds of social media magicians during this time brought on a large-scale following and the start of magical films and books surrounding the surrealism and mystery that magic creates. It also started the fascination with using technology to make the entertainment value higher and more alluring than ever before.

Magic Theories

What is important to remember when looking at the various theories that are rooted in magic, as well as where and how it originated, is the fact that even though magic is different now, the roots and theories surrounding its existence are part of the reason *why* it exists the *way* it exists now.

Each of these different theories discuss magic in different ways, and each of them has substantial evidence to prove and disprove their own statements, making magic as fluid as water.

Anthropological Theoretics

During the 1800s there was a common belief that magic was a 'pseudoscience,' which basically meant that the magic act would create a desired outcome. Sir Edward Burnett Tylor, however, vexed by magic, did not approach the subject as someone with superstitions but rather opted to study the concept and any phenomena that came paired with it. This allowed him to theorize that religion and magic generally came from the same system of thinking: they were not opposites or different systems of thinking but rather the same system of thinking, just viewed differently.

In his book *The Golden Bough*, Tylor concluded that magic, religion, and science were an evolutionary scheme, one where religion was preceded by magic because magic made logically more sense and was easier to understand. However, it was later found that Tylor made this assumption based on the fact that the Australian Aborigines had believed in magic and did not believe in religion.

Sociological Theoretical

French sociologists Èmile Durkheim and Marcel Mauss chose to define magic because of its social functionality. Durkheim believed that magic was used to manipulate singular objects to generate a specific outcome, and the ones manipulating the item were doing so for another person. What made this problematic was the fact that this meant there was not enough significance placed on the religious rites of that item, making the entire process one that was lacking motivation.

These ideas were furthered and supported by A. R Radcliffe-Brown in the text *The Andaman Islanders* (1922), as well as in Malinowski's *Argonauts of the Western Pacific* (1922). Radcliffe-Brown posited that magic was purely used to show the importance of a specific event, such as birthdays or funerals, while Malinowski posited that magic was an integral part of a person's psychological need for them to become a proper individual. This will be discussed more in the next section.

Upon further research and studies, Sir Edward Evans-Pritchard found that magic and religion were intertwined, and that magic was an important part of religion that could not be explained by the cultural differences and beliefs. This was mainly found in Africa and Oceanic areas.

For example, the Zande of Central Africa, believe in magic, witchcraft, and oracles. This is considered to be a normal part of their social and cultural structure. This was found to be so integrated that each part helps the other, keeping the entire system working, allowing for each action to have an opposite and equal reaction.

Psychological Theoretics

As mentioned above, Malinowski posited that magic was a part of an individual's psychological needs, and while the social and anthropological theories were justified in their own way, Malinowski felt that the psychological was far more important and true.

The most important views however resonated from Scottish Sociologist James George Frazer, who influenced Sigmund Freud's concept of what magic should be and was. Freud believed that there was some sort of psychological explanation for a belief in magic. He stated that the thoughts held by children, neurotics, and 'savages' all had one thing in common: they assumed that when they wished for something, their wish or their intention to have said item would lead them to getting that desire fulfilled. This, however, was revised and noted as an 'outmoded' view, as evidence was found to prove otherwise.

Claude Lévi-Strauss had initially also been ascribed to the three groups, but upon further investigation found that the structural linguistics of the time made the reasoning behind magic and its purposes different.

What very few people understand or seem to realize is that in the past, magic and religion were very closely correlated; many thought that a belief or knowledge meant that one used that as a reference for religion, and as such, that one could not have another belief structure.

What made magic so powerful was the fact that it created belief systems within religions. Ninian Smart had created a seven-dimensional worldview that made space for cross-cultural comparisons no matter their belief systems and religious views. The seven-dimensional map posited that religion was created out of the following seven things: Experiential, mythic, doctrinal, ethical, ritual, social, and material.

There are other methods that are often used to keep people from making comparisons between different belief systems. Jacob Neusner suggested that the modes be split into four different groupings: Magic, religion, science, and philosophy. This would allow people to make judgements and would keep comparatives split, allowing for better distinguishing between the different societies and their belief systems and religions.

One of the biggest problems that is fundamentally found during these times is the fact that different cultures would use magic for different reasons, and they would see magic in different ways. Consider that some would deem magic as bad and would shun those interested or partaking in it, sometimes even damning them to death because their views or interests were considered to be too wild or unknown, at times even considered witchcraft.

It is important to remember that this is where magic originally came from, something that was oftentimes excluded and looked down on, also sometimes misunderstood as being completely different to what it was (ie: 'deviltry' rather than something that could be logically explained). At its roots though one can assume that magic had always been something that was unknown and people wanted to know more. Still, the fear of the unknown was far too much for those who were complacent in their comfort zones.

Magic?

Now that the history and timelines have been reviewed, we can actually discuss the different types of magic that one can find and how those different magic categories are portrayed now and in the past.

As mentioned earlier, magic can be split into four subcategories, mainly: illusion, stage magic, close-up magic, and performance magic. There are of course other subgenres that can be classified, but that would mean deep diving into each category. These genres each have a way to entertain an audience through trickery, sleight of hand, or effects. It is important to separate these from paranormal magic, as there are differences between the two.

Illusion magic can be classified as magic that is done to create illusions by using different effects and skills to make something look different from reality. Tricks that include disappearing items that reappear somewhere else fall into the illusion category.

Stage magic is generally classified as tricks or stunts that could be performed on a stage. Anything from being blindfolded and using a knife to throw at a target to being able to use a card to cut through fruit would be classified as stage magic. Most modern magicians would fall into this category, as what they do would be seen as magic that is generally performed on a stage.

Close-up magic is defined as magic that happens right in front of your eyes. Generally, it is linked with sleight of hand as well as any card tricks, since you have to watch the magician's hands closely to be able to see what they are doing.

The final category, *performance magic* is something that includes stunts on a large scale. Something like diving off of a really high plank into a small pool on the ground would be considered performance magic. Often, the other categories can be put together to provide performance magic, creating an entire show surrounding different tricks and illusions.

Modern Magic

Magic has been revolutionized by many magicians in the last decades, and there are many modern magicians who have been part of this journey. There are hundreds of modern magicians that can be considered and looked at, as well as how their influence has changed the way we see magic today.

Those modern magicians include David Blaine, Penn & Teller, and Dynamo. David Blaine is most commonly known for his other-worldly stunts, some even commenting that it makes them uncomfortable to watch him. Penn & Teller is one of the more interesting acts, as Teller does not actually talk during their act at all or even in most interviews. Dynamo, on the other hand, is going back to the roots of magic, focusing on small sleight-of-hand tricks.

Later in this book, in Chapter 4, the most prominent modern magicians will be covered. This chapter will include their significant influence on modern magic and how they have traversed the changes that have come to magic over the last few years. Modern advancements have influenced magic in ways that we do not always fully understand or comprehend, and later in the book those concepts will be discussed.

THE FIRSTS

In this chapter the extensive history of the founding fathers of magic will be covered. Information regarding how they found their fame, skills, and knowledge came about is one of the most important aspects when it comes to their impact on modern magic history.

The era in which these four magicians lived and created magic is known as the "Golden Era of Magic." They created magnificent shows and would change the world of magic as we know it. They pushed the boundaries, never becoming comfortable in their place, always making sure to be ahead of the curve. They all had a passion for what they did. They truly were the best of the best.

The four magicians who will be covered in this section are the ones who started the magical journey we are on now. They revolutionized magic and were the leaders of their time. In later chapters, the modern magicians of the 21st century will be discussed, as well as their impact on our lives today and their involvement in how magic has changed and evolved.

Chapter 3 will cover the most important tricks that were shown and created by the magicians named in this section. These tricks will also be mentioned in Chapters 4 and 5 as a direct link to modern magic and the impact they had on modern magic.

Jean Eugène Robert-Houdin

Seen as the father of modern magical entertainment, Jean Eugène Robert-Houdin, was born in 1805 in Blois, France.

He was sent to University of Orlèans at the age of 11, his father hoping that he would become a lawyer, but instead he wanted to continue in his father's footsteps to become a clockmaker.

Unfortunately, by the time he returned from the university, Robert-Houdin's father had retired, so he then worked for his cousin for a few years. Robert-Houdin's skills as a clockmaker never disappeared, even after his love for illusion started.

Unknown author, Public domain, via Wikimedia Commons

Robert-Houdin's interest in clockmaking had started his career in illusionism, as he had ordered books for clockwork, but his books on clockwork were replaced by two volumes called *Scientific Amusement*. Instead of Robert-Houdin returning the books, he opted to study the new volumes and ended up reading them from front to back. This piqued his interest and he spent months learning and perfecting the techniques and skills that the books were describing.

Robert-Houdin kept studying horology and soon enough, he realized that the knowledge the books carried could only help him to an extent. As a way to improve, he paid an amateur entertainer to help him. Once Robert-Houdin was confident enough in his skills, he decided to move to Tours, where he started a watchmaking business and did basic entertainment and conjuring at fairs.

Jean Eugène Robert-Houdin was the first to open an entertainment area or magic theater in 1845, in Paris. He was backed by Count de l'Escalopier, who helped him finance the restructuring and rebuilding of the theater. He called the theater Palais Royale. After his first show, which Robert-Houdin had called "a failure," he wanted to close the theater, but after a friend's support he opted to keep it open. He continued to practice his skills and techniques but for an extended period of time very few people actually came to watch his shows.

About a year later, Robert-Houdin changed his set, adding a new trick to his repertoire, and he became increasingly popular. This allowed his popularity to grow and soon he could perform outside of his own theater, as well as alongside other magicians.

The trick that had made Jean Eugène Robert-Houdin popular was called 'second sight' (discussed in detail in the next chapter). While the title of the act was similar to magicians, such as John Henry Anderson, it was far more difficult. This trick was far more interesting than Anderson's as Robert-Houdin had included his son, Emile, in the trick, allowing his son to play a bigger role.

The only known information we have about Robert-Houdin is what we can find from his memoirs and notes; everything else seems rather hit or miss when it comes to the truthfulness of the information.

Unfortunately, Robert-Houdin's assistant, Le Grand, had stolen and copied many of his ideas and illusions, and they quickly became part of other magicians' sets, especially magicians like Alexander Herrmann and John Henry Anderson. There is no information stating that the other magicians had gotten the illusions from Le Grand himself or if they had sourced them from a third-party, but Le Grand was arrested for this.

Once the French Revolution ended the reign of Louis XVI, all Parisian theaters were closed. Jean Eugène Robert-Houdin closed Palais Royale and briefly went on tour through the country before moving to Britain. Louis-Napoleon III sent Robert-Houdin to Algeria, as he wanted the Algerian armies to know that French magic was stronger than their magical rituals. Upon completion of a special trick, by catching a marked bullet with his teeth, the mission was declared a success and he returned to his home in Saint-Gervais, near Bois, where he finished his memoirs, *Confidences d'un Prestigitateur*.

John Henry Anderson

John Henry Anderson, born in 1814 in Scotland, was one of the leading magicians who brought magic from street performing to theaters, allowing great magicians to give fantastic and entertaining performances all over.

dangoat https://www.flickr.com/photos/32409501@N07/,
Public domain, via Wikimedia Commons

He was orphaned at a young age, and began traveling with a dramatic company by the age of 16, in 1830. At 17, his performances in the magical arts began and at the young age of 23 he was one of the first to perform at Lord Panmure's castle. He settled in London in 1840, when he opened a theater, called the New Strand Theater. Here he performed his show *The Great Wizard of the North*, which was also a name bestowed upon him by Sir Walter Scott.

Unlike other magicians, Anderson found fame by advertising his shows; he exhibited great showmanship, and the capacity he had to advertise his shows made him world renowned. One of his most commonly known tricks was catching a bullet between his teeth; while he was not the one to invest the trick, it was one he executed perfectly, becoming one of the few magicians to be able to perform this trick masterfully.

Anderson was credited to be the first magician to pull a rabbit from a tophat. While he was not the one that thought of the premise of pulling an animal from a hat, he was the first to perform this version on stage.

While he had many children, all who helped him in his shows and tours, he found enough success to be able to fund and open a second theater. The City Theater in Glasgow came about in 1845. Unfortunately, the building burned down only a few months later and Anderson was almost left bankrupt. With the help of friends, however, he found himself being able to perform at the Covent Garden Theater in 1846.

Anderson toured most of Europe in 1847, doing shows in places like Hamburg, St. Petersburg, and Stockholm. After a chance meeting with Czar Nicolas I in St. Petersburg, Anderson returned to London in 1849. This was the year that he performed for Queen Victoria and Prince Albert. The year after, Anderson toured the United States, Canada, Australia, and Hawaii. Once he returned to the United Kingdom he found that Jean Eugène Robert-Houdin was now his rival.

Fortunately for him, Robert-Houdin's assistant had stolen most of his illusions and they were currently being used by multiple other magicians as well. Anderson returned to the United States in 1853 and performed Rober-Houdin's tricks. Unfortunately, one of the tricks he used, where he distributed alcohol to his audience, caused some issues and he decided to try out an acting career; soon after he did another tour and returned to England in 1864, upon realizing that he was greatly in debt.

At the age of 18, Anderson's son left his troupe, moving into conjuring. This left the father/son duo in shambles and they never spoke again after their last interaction. His death in 1874 was highlighted by the birth of Harry Houdini, who revered Anderson, naming him as one of his inspirations.

After his death, another magician by the name of Philip Prentis Hind, used Anderson's surname as a stage name, calling himself "Professor Anderson."

John Nevil Maskelyne

John Nevil Maskelyne was born to John Nevil Maskelyne senior and Harriet née Brundson in 1839 in Gloucestershire, England. Like Jean Eugène Robert-Houdin, he was trained in horology and watchmaking.

Unknown author, Public domain, via Wikimedia Commons

After watching a performance of the American Davenport Brothers at the local Town Hall, Maskelyne became interested in the occult and what magic had to offer. During their performance, Maskelyne had focused on the spirit cabinet illusion and stated during the performance that he would be able to recreate the exact illusion without having to use any occult or spiritual methods.

At a large gathering in 1865, Maskelyne and his friend George Alfred Cooke showcased a version of the Davenport Brothers' spirit box and explained how the brothers had created the illusion. The two men added elements of satire and comedy to the show, receiving much attention, causing them to perform the specific act various times.

Upon the positive feedback that the amateur magicians had found, they opted to travel with their show to neighboring towns, after which they found even more infamy. This encouraged their plans to become professional magicians.

Their tours seemed to be doing well but the two men struggled to make ends meet during the first tour. A manager, Willian Morton, offered to help them finance a tour, paying both John Nevil and his wife, as well as George Cooke. Their tours continued on for 2 years and finally ended at the Crystal Palace at the London Great Exhibition in 1851.

After their tour had finished, Morton had secured the duo a venue in Piccadilly, called the Egyptian Hall. After securing the building for the two, they renovated the hall and installed a stage before the grand opening in 1873. Morton continued to be their manager for almost 20 years after. They kept the hall for a whopping 31 years, performing there until its unfortunate demolition in 1905.

The two together were unstoppable: they created and built more tricks and illusions. Maskelyne was best known for his skills when it comes to the principles of illusion, mainly connected to levitation. Most commonly, it is believed that Jean Eugène Robert-Houdin was the inventor of the levitation illusion, but alas he was not. His form of levitation was far different than that of Maskelyne's. Various others believe that Harry Kellar, an American illusionist, was the inventor of levitation, but it was proved that he had bribed Maskelyne's technician for the information regarding the illusion.

The year 1905 marked a sad time for the duo as they not only lost Egyptian Hall but Maskelyne lost George Albert Cooke. Afterward, he made an agreement to work with David Devant. The two had first met in 1893 when Devant had auditioned to join the troupe but decided to go his own way.

Maskelyne was quite the author, and while he wrote and published various books, his most famous and well-known book was and still is *Sharps and Flats: A Complete Revelation of the Secrets of Cheating at Games of Chance and Skill.* This book highlighted and explained how one could win at any card or gambling game. While this was not the first of its kind, it was the first to be published by a recognized publishing house. This allowed the book to be more widely circulated, making it popular. To this day, the book is used by millions. It has been moved to an annotated website to make access easier.

Maskelyne, like Harry Houdini, was steadfast in his beliefs that the supernatural had no influence on illusions and magic, and in 1914 he founded The Occult Committee. This was a committee to investigate any claims that supernatural powers were being used to create illusions, as well as expose those claiming to be part of the supernatural, in turn exposing their fraud.

Maskelyne was constantly under fire by spiritualist Alfred Russel Wallace, who claimed that he had to have supernatural powers to be able to recreate the Davenport Brothers' spirit box illusion. He was part of various groups and committees that fought against the spiritual and supernatural. He sat in the Cambridge séances in 1895 for Eusapia Palladino, proving that she was not a medium.

While Maskelyne was active in the magic and illusion community and he loved what he did, he was also an avid inventor, creating what is known as the door lock for restrooms in London, where one would need to use a penny to be able to access the facilities.

Harry Houdini

Perhaps one of the most commonly known names when one thinks of magic is Harry Houdini. He was born Erik Weisz in 1874 and is most commonly known for his escape art as well as his illusionism.

Thurston, John H. (John Henry), 1852-, photographer, Public domain, via Wikimedia Commons

Houdini was born in Budapest, Hungary, to a Jewish mother and father called Cecilia Steiner and Mayer Sámuel Weisz. He was part of a family of nine, including his parents. He and his pregnant mother, father, and four brothers arrived in the United States in 1878. Upon entering the United States, they opted to change the spelling of their surname from the German spelling of Weisz to Weiss. They lived in Wisconsin, where his father was a rabbi and his mother stayed home to take care of the kids.

The 1880 census recorded that they lived on Appleton street. This area has now become known as the Houdini Plaza. In 1882, his father lost his job as rabbi and the family was forced to move to Milwaukee. He and his father moved to New York in 1887, and once his father had found a permanent job, the rest of the family joined them.

Houdini had various jobs as a youngster, being called the 'Prince of the Air' when he was a trapeze artist at the age of 9. Not only was he gymnastically talented but he was extremely athletically gifted, being a cross country champion runner when he was older.

Harry only became Harry Houdini once he started his career as a magician. Many believed that he had chosen the second name, Houdini, as an homage to Jean Eugène Robert-Houdin, but added an 'i' at the end as he believed that it was similar to the word 'like' in French dialects. Later in life, upon being asked about his name, Harry, he mentioned that it was an homage to Harry Kellar, who he had always admired as a youngster. Others however believed that it was adapted from 'Ehri,' which had been a nickname his family called him.

Houdini trained under the magician Joseph Rinn during his high school career at the Pastime Athletic Club. His magic career finally started in 1891, even though he was not very successful at the start. His performances included shows at museums, sideshows and even at some circuses. Houdini at first focused on sleight-of-hand card tricks, but finally he moved from card tricks to escapism. He performed alongside his brother Theodore "Dash," until the two of them met another performer, Wilhelmina Beatrice "Bess" Rahner. Dash was interested in Bess at first but in the end Harry and Bess were married, and she replaced Dash in the brothers' show. The show went from 'The Houdini Brothers' to 'The Houdinis.'

Houdini's career changed in 1899 when he took on a manager named Martin Beck, who advised him to stick to his escape acts. Martin Beck found Houdini a spot on the Orpheum Vaudeville circuit, and within months he was performing at some of the top houses in Vaudeville.

Houdini's first European tour was in 1900, and upon some unsuccessful interviews, the British manager Houdini had, Harry Day, found him an interview with C. Dundas Slater, the then manager of the Alhambra Theater. This led to an introduction to William Melville, allowing him to give a demonstration of how he escaped handcuffs at Scotland Yard. This show was so successful that he was booked at the theater for 6 months.

His fame grew and between 1900 and 1920 Houdini showcased his escape arts in various theaters all over Great Britain; these shows included illusions, cards tricks, and various stunts that were performed outdoors. This made him one of the most successful and highest paid entertainers in the world. The success allowed Houdini to travel through Europe, seeing places like Germany, France, and Russia. During his tour he would challenge local law enforcement to lock him up in their jails. One of his most interesting of these was when he was locked on a Siberian transport van, stating that he would need to go to Siberia where the key was if he was unable to escape.

Houdini returned to the United States in 1904, when he finally settled, buying a home for himself and his family. In 1906 he started his own publication, *Conjurers' Monthly Magazine*, but unfortunately it only lasted for two publications as it turned into a platform for Houdini to attack his rivals and changed some historical information to fit his view of magic and what magic was supposed to be.

From 1907 to the early 1910s Houdini found great success in his performances in the United States, but upon various other magicians copying his handcuff escape technique, he retired the act in

1908, and transitioned to an escape trick where he would escape from a water-filled milk can. There was more danger and possibility of failure when it came to this specific act. Houdini opted to expand his repertoire by asking members of his audience to create contraptions and ideas to hold him. One of the most interesting of these was the Brewers in Scranton, who suggested that Houdini escape a barrel after it was filled with beer. Other suggestions were mail bags and even a whale that had washed up on shore in Boston.

In 1908 a collection of articles written by Houdini, titled *The Unmasking of Robert-Houdin*, was published, outlining the history of magic up until then. He also used the book to discredit Robert-Houdin, stating that he was fraudulent in his creation of the automata and various parts of his shows like aerial suspension. Jean Hugard responded to Houdini's book by writing a full rebuttal, decrediting all Houdini had said.

Houdini introduced a varying array of different escapes during his entire career, adding the 'Chinese Water Torture Cell' in 1912. Houdini did, however, explain some of his basic handcuff tricks in books that were written for the magic brotherhood. These books were titled *Handcuff Secrets* and were published in 1909.

Houdini did try to follow an acting career, but found no real success there. He was featured in one full-length film called *The Grim Game*. This film was lost but it was discovered that a collector had the last copy of the film. It took Dick Brookz and Dorothy Dietrich, who owned the Houdini Museum, a few years to convince the collector to sell it to them and after a while he did. The film was restored and in 2015 the film was shown by Turner Classic Movies during their 4-day festival in Hollywood.

Aviation was also a part of Houdini's fascinations and he bought a French Voisin biplane in 1909. One of his goals was to be the first to fly in Australia, but after some proper investigation it was found that Colin Defries was the first to fly in 1909, a year before Houdini had made his first flight there. Houdini settled somewhat before he finally turned his energy and efforts towards the debunking of psychics and mediums. This was similar to the rest of the stage magicians of the time.

Houdini's magical knowledge allowed him to expose and devalue those mediums that had fooled both scientists and various academics. As an integral part of the Scientific American committee, he took it upon himself to help to expose phonies, and this just fueled and inspired others to do the same. Houdini chose to chronicle his exposing exploits in a book called *A Magician Among the Spirits*. The book was said to be co-authored by C. M. Eddy Jr, but he was never credited.

After his death, Houdini's wife would hold a séance on Halloween, after the couple had agreed that he would try and communicate with her via a secret code between the two. After 10 years his wife stopped doing the séance but memorial séances are held all over the world every year, the first official Houdini séance being held in the 1940s.

This might seem odd as Houdini spent most of his career fighting against the supernatural, trying to debunk seances and the like. It is believed that Houdini and his wife agreed to do this ritual as a way to prove that the supernatural did not exist.

Houdini died of peritonitis as well as a ruptured appendix. Houdini's death is surrounded by some mystery as some believe that Jocelyn Gordon Whitehead was speculated to be responsible for his death. There were rumors that Jocelyn had repeatedly hit Houdini's abdomen in his dressing room in the Princess Theater. While this seems odd, Houdini had an act where he would prove that he could withstand any hard punch. Whitehead had asked if he could punch Houdini. Houdini had agreed but before he could stand up from the couch where he had been resting Whitehead had punched him, not giving Houdini the time he normally needed to prepare for the blow, both mentally and physically.

Houdini's assistant gave a recount of the incident, telling of the interaction between Houdini and Whitehead. Houdini had gone to a doctor a few days later, being told to have surgery but choosing not to. He continued with his shows, and after having passed out and being revived at a show was hospitalized after the show ended. Houdini's insurance company deemed his cause of death to be due to the incident in Houdini's dressing room and thus paid his wife double the indemnity.

A statuary bust was added to his gravesite, a rarity as Jewish gravesites did not often allow such. Unfortunately, the bust was destroyed by various vandals and until 2011 temporary busts were placed on Houdini's grave. In 2011 a group, calling themselves Houdini Commando's, who worked at the Houdini Museum in Pennsylvania, replaced the temporary busts with a permanent one, after having received permission from both his family and the cemetery.

MAGIC TRICK HISTORY

In this chapter various tricks from the first magicians will be covered. I will be referencing some of the magicians in Chapter 2, including basic insight and notation surrounding the tricks and how these magicians accomplished the tricks and illusions they did.

Jean Eugène Robert-Houdin

Robert-Houdin had various tricks, some he started out with and some he chose to perfect, each of them extremely important to his career, and the evolution of magic to where it is now.

Second Sight

This was Robert-Houdin's first major trick. This was the trick that interested people and made him far more popular than he used to be. He devised this trick to intrigue people to attend more of his shows.

This would be a duo act, where one would be reading the other's mind. Robert-Houdin had a story about his son Emile creating a game of hot and cold that he would use as a basis for his trick.

While the trick had the same name as those of other magicians, like John Henry Anderson, the trick itself was different. While Anderson had a box where he would place items inside and then someone would describe the items, Robert-Houdin's version was slightly different. He would wander into the audience and touch a random object that an audience member was holding up, and his son, who was blindfolded, would describe each object.

After a while the method to this trick changed and Robert-Houdin opted to ring a bell, instead of asking his son what the item was. This made the trick seem far more interesting as there was no actual communication between the two. He would place the bell down and his son would again describe the items in great detail.

Later on Robert-Houdin opted to make the trick even more complex. He placed a cup of water in his son's hands and his son would taste the water and then describe whatever the audience member was thinking of. Some were so shocked and intrigued that in order to change things the audience members would bring items like thread counters and books that were written in different languages.

The Ethereal Suspension

AnonymousUnknown author, Public domain, via Wikimedia Commons

Throughout his performance career, there were constant conversations surrounding the use of ether in performances. Robert-Houdin opted to use the foul-smelling liquid. He used the premise and explained to his audience that when the liquid is inhaled in its highest form, the body of the person inhaling it will become weightless for a few seconds, similar to a balloon.

To prove this, Robert-Houdin placed three wooden chairs on a wooden bench, letting his youngest son stand on the one in the middle. His son, Eugène, put his arms out straight, as instructed by his father and Robert-Houdin placed canes underneath his arms, on top of the other chairs.

Robert-Houdin proceeded to open the bottle of ether and the entire audience could smell the horrid gas wafting through the theater. He held the vial underneath Eugène's nose and his entire body went limp; however, in reality the vial was empty and the smell was coming from behind the stage where Robert-Houdin's eldest son, Emile, was pouring ether over a hot shovel to create the gas in a way to waft through the theater.

Slowly but surely Robert-Houdin took away the chair his son was standing on, then took away one cane: his son was now hanging on by one arm. Slowly, he lifted his son into an upright position and then pulled his hand away, letting his son be suspended in the air, to prove that the trick worked, he stepped away from his son, only letting his son balance by his elbow.

Once he knew that the ether would be wearing off, Robert-Houdin repositioned his son back into the position he was in originally and everything seemed perfectly fine with Eugène. After Robert-Houdin had made a comment about how the ether might 'combust' various protests were heard by audience members, stating that he was putting his son's life at risk.

The Marvelous Orange Tree

This was a popular trick that Robert-Houdin loved to perform. He would have a small side table with an egg, a lemon, and an orange on it. He would wander into the audience and select an audience member whose handkerchief he would borrow. Slowly he would roll the handkerchief into a ball and it would become smaller and smaller until it could pass through the egg that was on the table.

Robert-Houdin would pick up the egg, and as common sense dictates, people assumed he would break open the egg and make the handkerchief reappear, but instead he would make the egg disappear as well. He would tell the audience that the egg had gone inside the lemon. The process continued until he came to the orange, which only left a powder in its wake. The powder was then placed in a vial, which he soaked in alcohol and then set on fire.

An orange tree he had planted earlier that had already started growing was brought to the stage by one of his assistants, and he would point out how the tree had no flowers or fruits. The vial, still on fire, would be placed underneath the tree and the vapor from the burning vial would cause the tree to blossom both flowers and orange blossoms. To make this more of a show, Robert-Houdin would pick up a wand and as he waved it the flowers would disappear and oranges would take their place.

No matter how many oranges there were, Robert-Houdin would pluck the oranges and send them into the audience so people would be able to tell that they were real, all of them except one. He would again wave his wand and the only orange left would be split into four, revealing a white fabric. Two butterflies, constructed from clockwork items, would move from behind the tree and each grab a corner of the fabric and spread it open, revealing the handkerchief from the audience member. This trick was used in the film *The Illusionist* in 2006, but the trick in the movie was made a little more complex.

Harry Houdini

Harry Houdini was a wonderful magician and while he is one of the most commonly known magicians in the world, there is a great reason for that. Not only were the stunts he did dangerous and reckless, but he loved doing them.

Daily Mirror Challenge

Houdini was challenged in 1904 by the London *Daily Mirror* to escape from handcuffs that had been specifically made to not be escapable, by a locksmith from Birmingham. Houdini of course accepted the challenge and performed the stunt on March 17th in front of 4,000 people during a performance at the Hippodrome Theater.

Houdini's escape attempt lasted for more than an hour, and after a while he asked if they could remove the cuffs to be able to take off his jacket, but the representative that had been sent from the *Daily Mirror* declined, stating that Houdini might get an edge on how to escape if he saw how the cuffs were unlocked. After about 50 minutes, his wife appeared on stage, kissing him; many speculated that she had brought him the key in this manner, but this theory has been proven wrong due to the fact that the key was 6 inches long.

After another hour he appeared fully on stage again, this time free. The crowd was both shocked and amazed, and as he was celebrated by the crowd, and journalists he started crying, stating that it had been the most difficult escape he had made. What made this trick so much more interesting was the fact that Houdini had performed most of the trick behind a screen. It was quite common for magicians that did escape acts to do this, as to keep an air of mystery surrounding their escape. While they could not be seen, because of the screen, they were still theoretically on the stage the whole time.

Various different accounts exist of what actually happened during that escape. A close friend stated that he could not escape and that he had his wife ask the *Daily Mirror* representative for the key. However, there is no actual evidence of what truly happened, as Houdini had remained 'hidden' behind a screen that would keep people from seeing him escape.

Milk Can Escape

In 1908, Houdini debuted his own creation, the Milk Can Escape. The act included Houdini handcuffed inside an oversized milk can that was sealed and filled with water. As part of his escape Houdini would often challenge audience members to hold their breath alongside him to see if they would be able to escape the situation. The posters that circulated read "Failure Means A Drowning Death," which only sensationalized his act more and he became extremely popular.

Once this was no longer entertaining enough, Houdini added to the escape that the can be locked inside a wooden chest that would be wrapped in chains and locked using a padlock. For 4 years Houdini performed this trick regularly as part of his routine, and it has been one of his most prominent tricks.

The Milk Can and the Overboard Box can be seen in the American Museum of Magic.

Chinese Water Torture Cell

Because so many other magicians had started copying and imitating the Milk Can Escape, Houdini changed the act, replacing the Milk Can with a Chinese Water Torture Cell.

https://lccn.loc.gov/96518829, Public domain, via Wikimedia Commons

Houdini would be locked in stocks by his feet and would be lowered into a tank filled with water, while also being upside down. The stocks attached to his feet would be locked to the water tank. When Houdini first started the escape he would let them lower a metal cage into the water that surrounded him. The cage would leave less space for movement and would not let Houdini turn, while also offering some safety if the glass were to break.

Houdini first performed the escape in England, where the props had been constructed. He had titled it "Houdini Upside Down," which allowed him to add a copyright to the trick, allowing him to sue and take legal action against any who would copy or imitate him. The escape was always called the Chinese Water Torture Cell, or The Water Torture Cell, but Houdini referred to it as the Upside Down.

The first official and public performance of the Upside Down took place in Berlin, during a Circus Busch performance in 1912. Houdini continued to perform the Upside Down until he died in 1926.

Suspended Straitjacket Escape

One of Houdini's most publicly known tricks was to be suspended by his ankles from a building or a crane while also being strapped in a straitjacket. He would always perform this while there were many onlookers, not having any sort of cover or screen to keep people from seeing his escape method.

Houdini would often perform the trick from the office of a local newsroom, allowing him all the press coverage he could ask for. He had once performed the trick on one of the cranes that was being used to build the subway. The entire trick took Houdini 2 minutes and 37 seconds, from the first movement to when the straitjacket was off. The Library of Congress has film footage of this feat and you can also see films of his various escapes at The Houdini Museum in Pennsylvania.

Visible safety wire had been added to his ankles when strong winds had caused Houdini various injuries, due to being slammed against the building he was performing the trick on. These wires would allow for Houdini to be pulled away from the building if it was necessary.

Houdini had Randolph Osborne Douglas to thank for the idea of the Straitjacket Escape. He and the boy had met at the Sheffield's Empire Theater, and the boy had spoken about the idea with Houdini.

Overboard Box Escape

The first time Houdini escaped from the overboard box was in 1912 in the New York East River. He would be lowered in the water, after the crate had been roped and nailed shut.

Police had told him that he was not allowed to do so from piers and this resulted in Houdini renting a tugboat to help him pull off this trick. Houdini had also invited press onto the boat to see him escape.

Dietz, Carl, photographer, Public Domain, Library of Congress

Houdini was locked in handcuffs and added leg irons to make it more challenging before getting into the crate that was nailed shut, roped around, and then weighed down by weights totaling up to 200 pounds.

The crate was then lowered into the water. The first time Houdini escaped in 57 seconds.

The crate had been found to have no actual breaking points and the irons and handcuffs were found inside.

Houdini had also performed this act on stage, once at Hamerstein's Roof garden and then at the New York Hippodrome.

To be able to do this he used a 5,500 US-gallon tank that had been specifically built for the trick to be replicated on stage.

Buried Alive

While this was a popular act to do, Houdini had changed and varied the buried alive trick at least three different times.

Otis Lithograph Co., Library of Congress

The first time was in 1915, where he almost lost his life. The trick took place in Santa Ana, California, where he was buried without a box or casket, underneath 6 feet of ground. After a while, he started getting tired and panicked as he dug to the surface. The moment his hand had reached the surface and he could no longer feel more ground above him, he passed out, and ultimately had to be pulled from the earth. It was later noted that Houdini felt this was one of his more dangerous acts.

The second variant that Houdini had done was merely a way to expose another performer by the name of Rahman Bey. Rahman had stated that he used supernatural powers to be able to stay in an enclosed box for an hour. Houdini wanted to challenge him and on August 5th, 1926, Houdini bested Rahman Bey by being sealed in a casket for 90 minutes. The casket was sealed and lowered into the swimming pool at the New York Shelton Hotel. Later the same year, Houdini recreated the trick in Massachusetts at the local YMCA in Worcester, when he remained sealed in a casket for 71 minutes.

Houdini's final variation of the buried-alive trick would be featured in a show where he would be strapped in a straitjacket, sealed in a casket, and then buried inside a tank that would be filled with sand. The show was scheduled for his first season in 1927. There is no actual evidence that shows that Houdini ever performed the buried-alive trick on stage and since he passed away in 1926, before he could perform the third variation, the bronze casket that had been made for the trick was used to transport his body from Detroit to New York.

MODERN MAGICIANS

This section will cover six of the most commonly known modern magicians and how their history has paved the way for modern magic. This section will mainly cover their backgrounds, as Chapter 5 will cover their illusions and shows.

David Copperfield

Originally born David Seth Kotkin in 1956, David Copperfield has been named the most successful magician in history.

Homer Liwag, CC BY-SA 4.0, via Wikimedia Commons

His shows have won 21 Emmy Awards, he has broken 11 Guinness World Records, and he has a star on the Hollywood Walk of Fame.

David Copperfield was born in New Jersey, to Jewish parents. At the age of 10 his magical career started, as he went around the neighborhood performing as 'Davino the Boy Magician.' At the age of 12, in 1968, he was the youngest person to ever be invited and admitted to the Society of American Magicians.

Copperfield attended Camp Harmony, a magic camp where he could practice his skills and learn ventriloquism. His teenage years were filled with his fascination with Broadway, and he is known to have snuck into a few magic shows during these times. Copperfield was so popular that at the age of 16, in 1971 he was teaching a magic course at the New York University.

Copperfield attended college at the Fordham University in New York but 3 weeks later chose to drop out to play the lead role for a Broadway production, called *The Magic Man*. Upon his move to Chicago he adopted the stage name David Copperfield, which is speculated to have been inspired by the Charles Dickens novel of the same name. This Broadway show became the longest running musical in Chicago history.

At the young age of 19, he starred in his first show, called *Magic of David Copperfield* in Hawaii; the show ran for a few months thanks to the help of Willy Martin, a sound and lighting designer Copperfield had worked with before. Copperfield did not stop though; in 1977 he was cast as the host for *The Magic of ABC* after being discovered by Joseph Crates, a popular producer for both television series and Broadway shows.

Between 1978 and 2001, Copperfield hosted multiple specials called *The Magic of David Copperfield* on CBS. Between 1977 and 2001 there were approximately 2 documentaries and 19 David Copperfield specials. Copperfield also acted in other films, such as *Terror Train* in 1980, *Statue of Liberty* in 1983, and *Alcatraz Prison* in 1987.

One of Copperfield's more famous illusions has to be the 1983 disappearance of the Statue of Liberty. The year 1996 marked another fantastic feat for Copperfield, as his show *Dreams & Nightmares* had broken box office records at the Martin Beck Theater (now the Al Hirschfeld Theater) in New York City.

Copperfield also published his first book in 1996: titled *David Copperfield's Tales of the Impossible*, the book was brought to life with the help of Dean Koontz, Ray Bradbury, and Joyce Carol Oats. The second volume of the book, titled *David Copperfield's Beyond Imagination*, was published in 1997.

In 2001 Copperfield performed at the White House for the UNICEF benefit, where the actress and singer Jennifer Lopez was cut into six pieces. He was invited to do an hour-long biography series in 2002.

Copperfield was constantly in the public eye, creating illusions as he went, and in 2009 he made his first live television appearance during his performance at the 44th Annual Academy of Country Music Awards. He only performed two illusions, one sawing singer and songwriter Taylor Swift in half and the other making her appear in an empty elevator.

The year 2009 also marked a small scandal, when he was supposedly dropped by Michael Jackson after some disagreements over money and payment, but the truth of the matter was never revealed.

The news of the collaboration between Jackson and Copperfield was first released on the 1st of April in 2009, and many believe it to have been just an April Fools joke.

Copperfield started his Australian tour in 2009, and after finishing his tour, joined the cast for a film titled *Burt Wonderstone* in 2011. In 2012 he was part of a special and interview as part of *Oprah's Next Chapter*.

Flag Day 2019 marked a wonderful day for all when Copperfield made a missing star on the Star-Spangled Banner reappear. It is believed that the missing star had been removed from this flag in the 19th century.

It is important to note that Copperfield has mentioned that his heroes and role models were never other magicians but rather artists, like Walt Disney and Fred Astaire.

He noted that this was because he wanted to create an art form rather than just creating basic illusions or shows.

James Randi

Randall James Hamilton Zwinge was born in 1928 in Ontario, Canada. He had two younger siblings, a brother and a sister.

Sgerbic, CC BY-SA 4.0, via Wikimedia Commons

His fascination with magic started after he had seen Harry Blackstone Senior, which led him to reading various conjuring novels. This happened after he had been in a bicycle accident at the age of 13 and he was in a body cast.

At the age of 17 he dropped out of high school to be part of a traveling carnival show. He also practiced mentalist acts in various nightclubs, as well as at the Canadian National Exhibition. In his teenage years he also came across a church where the pastor had claimed to be able to read minds, but after he had duplicated the trick to the parishioners, the pastor's wife had called the police, resulting in the pastor spending some time in jail. This incident fueled James to become a skeptic, one that was skeptical of those claiming to have supernatural powers.

Randi used his early 20s to pose as an astrologer, writing an astrological column for the *Midnight* tabloid, pointing out how they were merely doing simple tricks by copying and shuffling around other columns and putting them together. His 30s were his traveling years as he worked in United Kingdom, Philippine, and European nightclubs, as well as those in Japan, using this as a way to witness entertainers who stated that they were using supernatural powers.

Randi first started his career as a escapologist and stage magician in 1946, generally focusing on escape acts from prison cells and safes all around the world. Randi's most popular feat was the televization of him being locked and sealed in a coffin for 104 minutes inside a hotel swimming pool, beating Houdini's time of 93 minutes.

Randi was a guest on the *Long John Nebel Show*, which aired on New York City radio, and often did character voices for commercials; however, after Nebel moved to a different station Randi took over Nebel's time slot at the radio and started airing a show called *The Amazing Randi* show between 1967 and 1968. The show was focused on having guests who would defend any and all paranormal claims. The show ended because of discourse between the archbishop of New York and Randi.

The Amazing Randi also appeared on the children's series *Wonderama*, often between 1959 and 1967, while also hosting various television specials and traveling the world for tours. During the *Billion Dollar Babies* tour hosted by Alice Cooper, Randi played both the mad dentist and the executioner, while also having helped build some of the stage props. There have been consistent claims that Randi is actually a psychic or supernatural, but Randi has always denied the claims, stating clearly that he was using trickery and illusion to create the shows and entertainment he was showcasing.

Randi, like most others, was an author as well as a magician. In 1992 he published a book titled *Conjuring*, a look at the most prominent magicians in history. Randi also published a visual and illustrated biography called *Houdini, His Life and Art*, which was co-authored with Beth Sugar. The book documented Houdini's professional and private life.

Randi published a children's book titled *The Magic World of Amazing Randi* in 1989, while also publishing various educational novels surrounding paranormal and pseudoscientific claims. Randi's writing and disagreement with paranormals really became popular in 1972 when he challenged Uri Geller publicly by calling him a fraud, stating that Geller was using basic illusion and magic tricks instead of the paranormal feats Gellar had stated to be using. These arguments can be found in *The Truth about Uri Geller*, which was published in 1982.

In 1986 Randi was awarded the MacArthur Foundation Fellowship, and a grant of $272,000 was awarded to him to help him with his investigations into faith healers, some of whom were W. V. Grant, Ernest Angley, and Peter Popoff. Randi exposed most of them on *The Tonight Show Starring Johnny Carson* in the same year.

David Blaine

David Blaine was born in 1973 in New York to a single mother who was a teacher.

David Shankbone, CC BY-SA 3.0, via Wikimedia Commons

His obsession and interest in magic began when he saw a magician perform on the subway, at the young age of 4. He moved multiple times as a young teenager and lost his mother at a young age, having to fend for himself.

When he was 24, Blaine's first television show, *David Blaine: Street Magic*, was aired on ABC. The show took the world by storm, making it successful enough for two more similar shows to be created. The show's premise was based on Blaine traveling across the country and performing his street art. The producer made commentary that the show was not about Blaine but rather about the raw emotions and reactions of those Blaine was entertaining.

Blaine upped the ante in 1999 when he was enclosed in a plastic tank, beneath a 3-ton tank that was filled with water. The duration of the stunt was to be for 7 days. The groups of people that came the day when he emerged from the tank were astonished and news outlets made statements claiming that he had done better than his role model, Houdini.

Blaine had various other feats during his career but like many before him, he also delved into writing. He helped publish an autobiography titled *Mysterious Stranger: A Book of Magic* in 2002. The book was also a mystery that readers could solve. Sherri Skanes solved the puzzle in 2004.

Blaine is also a big philanthropist, as well as a charity worker. He performed for The Salvation Army in 2006, and performed a charity event called *Magic for Haiti* after the Hatian earthquake in 2010. He even continued his hospital shows over Zoom and Face-Time in 2020 due to the COVID pandemic.

Criss Angel

Criss Angel, born Christopher Nicholas Sarantakos in 1967, began his magical career in New York.

Thomas Rutan, CC0, via Wikimedia Commons

He is most commonly known for his hosting role in *Criss Angel: Mindfreak,* and the earlier live performance *Criss Angel Believe* that was part of a show with Cirque du Soleil in Las Vegas.

His interest in magic started at age 7, and after a few years of practice he did his first show at the age of 12. He was paid $10 for his performance. He continued his training and by the time he was 14 he was performing in restaurants all over the area where he lived.

When he finished high school, Angel decided that he wanted to entirely dedicate his time and career to being a professional magician instead of going to college. He decided to travel with different groups, taking time to study at local libraries to further his knowledge surrounding magic and the history behind it.

He first appeared on a show called *Secrets* in 1994. This started his television career, lining up his first performance at the *World of Illusion* conference in 1998 at Madison Square Garden in New York City. The year 1997 marked his first television film, titled *The Science of Magic*; he also played a major role in the sequel, *The Science of Magic II*, which was released in 2003. While *Criss Angel: Mindfreak* was an off-Broadway show that had been picked up by World Underground Theater, it became Angel's first television series. Between the years of 2001 and 2003 more than 600 performances were done by Angel at the World Underground Theater in Time Square, New York. One of Angel's best known records was when he spent 24 hours in a water tank. This broke a world record, for a human being completely submerged in water, and also later became a part of his television show.

Angel was part of various shows between the years of 2002 and 2005. He performed all over the country, as well as taking part in various specials and interviews surrounding his performances and skills. The *Criss Angel: Mindfreak* series was successful enough to warrant three different seasons for the show. The show was successful enough that it brought a resurgence of popularity to magic and its accompanying aspects and successfully ran from 2005 until 2010.

Besides his televised show, Angel also performed in a stage production called *Criss Angel: Believe*. The show was partnered with Cirque du Soleil, set in Las Vegas at the Luxor. At the start, the show received multiple mediocre reviews, and while the show got better, the 2009 rendition of the show ended with Angel insulting a blogger after hearing that the blogger had been commenting on social media during the show.

The show continued to be hosted each year and had a 10-year contract to be produced through 2019 as well. The show was the best-selling magic show in the year 2013. Along with the various shows, Angel was also a judge on the show *Phenomenon*, where his main goal was to disprove anyone who said they had any form of supernatural abilities or powers.

Criss Angel was also a part of other projects surrounding music, merchandising, as well as authoring a book. In 2007 *Mindfreak: Secret Revelations* was released by HarperEntertainment, and it reached the *Los Angeles Times* bestseller list. The book includes images as well as some step-by-step instructions of some of the more basic tricks he does. Angel had the help of writer Laura Morton to help author the book.

Derren Brown

Derren Brown was born in 1971 in Croydon, London.

Garry Knight, CC BY 2.0, via Wikimedia Commons

He was in a private school and went on to study German as well as Law at the University of Bristol. His love of magic and illusion started when he attended a hypnosis show hosted by Martin Taylor. The show moved him so much that he felt the need to shift his career from law and German to hypnosis and illusions. During his undergraduate year at the university, he started performing at bars and restaurants, only doing close-up magic. His first stage performance was at the University of Bristol in 1992 and he performed under the stage name Darren 'V' Brown.

Brown has stated various times that his success was due to Jerry Sadowitz, who had helped him get in touch with H&R Publishers and Objective Productions, who helped him secure his television show, *Mind Control*, in 2000. After the success of his own shows, he started his own production company, called Vaudeville Productions, that would allow him to produce more productions for himself as well as with other performers.

Brown was also an author to various books surrounding magic and illusion. In his book *Tricks of the Mind*, Brown explains concepts like cold reading. He mentioned this while being part of the two-part special *The Enemies of Reason*, in 2009. Other books include *Pure Effect*, *Happy*, *Absolute Magic*, and *Confessions of a Conjuror*.

Brown has been known to make controversial statements, and thus his shows have been surrounded by controversy. One of the shows, called *Russian Roulette*, found itself constantly critized for its lack of taste, some saying that it was a way to make light of suicide and that it advocated for bad gun control. There had also been police warnings submitted to the show stating that copycat acts might occur.

Brown has stated that he uses various methods to do his hypnosis and illusions. He mainly uses memory techniques, body language reading, and cognitive psychology, as well as cold reading and subliminal psychology. Once asked about his knowledge surrounding psychology, he stated that he knew the skills, he just did not know how to apply that knowledge until he started doing close-up magic. He was also asked about being able to detect when people were lying, to which he responded that he purely knew how to read micro-muscle movements that would indicate if someone was lying or not.

Penn & Teller

Unlike all the other magicians in this list, Penn & Teller are a duo.

Garry Knight, CC BY 2.0, via Wikimedia Commons

Penn Jillette and Raymond Joseph Teller are illusionists and skeptics who have been working together since the 1970s, mainly combining magic and comedy during their shows. The two met each other due to a common friend, Wier Chrisemer, and they had their first-ever duo performance in 1975. From 1975 to 1981, Penn & Teller performed alongside Chrisemer as "The Asparagus Cultural Society." Chrisemer had helped the duo create some of their most iconic tricks and in 1981 the trio disbanded after Chrisemer quit show business. Penn & Teller however, continued their show as a duo, now called "Mrs. Lonsberry's Seance of Horror."

What made Penn & Teller one of the most interesting acts to behold was the fact that only one of the duo spoke. Teller never articulated or spoke during their shows, making him essentially mute. Teller will mime during their performance, while Penn would be the orator. This made their shows that much more entertaining, especially since they would expose other tricks and stunts in entertaining and fun ways.

In 1985 the duo had received many positive reviews because of their special, *Penn & Teller Go Public*. In 1987 they started the first of three Broadway shows, and also appeared in a music video by Run-DMC. From the late 1980s through the early 1990s they made various appearances on shows like *Late Night with David Letterman* as well as *Saturday Night Live*, *Late Night with Conan O'Brien*, and *Today*.

The 1990s marked Penn & Teller's national tours. This also included all of the appearances they made on various television shows, including *The Drew Carey Show*, *Muppets Tonight*, *The West Wing*, and *The Simpsons*. They also made an appearance in Katy Perry's music video for the song *Waking Up in Vegas* in 2009, as well as being featured in an episode on *Bill Nye the Science Guy*.

Penn & Teller hosted a show called *Bullshit!* from 2003 to 2010 that focused on the skepticism surrounding not only psychics but also religion, conspiracy theories, and paranormal acts. The show has covered various topics, the most prominent being gun control, environmental issues, PETA, the Americans with Disabilities Act, as well as the war on drugs.

Like most, the two have authored various books on magic, and Penn has also released various books by himself. Teller also authored by himself, although he only wrote one book, titled *When I'm Dead All This Will Be Yours: Joe Teller - A Portrait by His Kid*.

While the two work together wonderfully, they have only a few things in common besides magic, and while they have a fantastic working relationship, it is said that the two rarely spend time together in social situations outside of their work and performances. However, during an interview, Penn had stated that Teller was and is his best friend and that they treated each other like family.

The interview continued where they spoke of the common respect and trust they have for each other, and how their relationship is different from other duos because they do not spend excessive amounts of time together. Later, during an interview for NPR, Teller had said that even if they did disagree, that it would ultimately lead to better decisions regarding their art as it would allow them to think outside the box.

In 2013 the pair received recognition for their hard work, receiving a star on the Hollywood Walk of Fame. The star is located a few stars away from both Harry Houdini's star and *The Magic Castle*. They have also garnered other rewards in their years as a duo, including a Writers Guild of America award for their show *Penn & Teller: Bullshit!*

The duo has also been nominated for 11 Emmy Awards, actually winning an award in 1985 for their show *Penn & Teller Go Public*. In 2017 they were nominated for a Critic's Choice Award for their show *Penn & Teller: Fool Us* and 2003 was the year that they received the Emperor Has No Clothes Award. This award mainly focuses on the shortcomings of religion in public figures. They also received the Richard Dawkins Award in 2005 and the Hugh M. Hefner First Amendment Award.

In 2014 they were nominated for a BAFTA for the documentary they created, titled *Tim's Vermeer*, and in 2020 they received a nomination for an Oliver Award for their contribution on the show *Magic Goes Wrong*.

Dynamo

Born in 1982 as Steven Frayne, the British magician made waves across the world with his traveling shows and illusions.

His stage name, Dynamo, was something that had been given to him by an audience member during a performance at the New York Hilton, during a centenary celebration for Harry Houdini. Others that attended the show were David Copperfield and David Blaine. The audience member had shouted out that he was "a dynamo" and the name stuck; Dynamo has been making waves as an amazing magician since.

Dynamo started his career in 2003 when he was awarded a loan from the Prince's trust. This would allow him to invest in camera equipment so he could record his performances. He had lived in Bradford, West Yorkshire and moved to London in 2004 to start pursuing his career in magic.

Walterlan Papetti, CC BY-SA 4.0, via Wikimedia Commons

Dynamo's plan of action was to film a collection of his tricks and publish them. With a camera man and a few other team members, he set out to film himself to impress others. He would mostly perform in the streets of London but oftentimes he would impress doormen that would allow him backstage at certain events, allowing him to perform for artists like Coldplay, Snoop Dogg, and Gwyneth Paltrow. This garnered him lots of attention, and the added fame he had found on YouTube from posting his clips sent him skyrocketing into fame and fortune.

What made Dynamo different from the other magicians of his time was the fact that he focused on sleight of hand and small illusions rather than spending time building elaborate tricks and spending hours without food. He focused on what he was good at.

His first television appearance was in 2002 on the show *Richard & Judy*. Directors and various executives had been so impressed with his skill and work that they paid for him to take part in a 1-hour special documentary, titled *Dynamo's Estate of Mind*. The show consisted of a camera crew following him around while he toured London and did the very magic that had made him famous.

The very first show that was his own, titled *Dynamo: Magician Impossible*, aired for the first time in July 2011. The show was successful enough to create more seasons, the second season airing in July 2012. The third series was filmed and aired in July 2013 and the fourth and final season aired in September 2014. Each season Dynamo would travel to different cities and do his magic for various onlookers, allowing them to watch his skill up close. People were amazed at his skills and all four seasons were nominated for various awards.

In 2016 Dynamo released an hour-long documentary, titled *Dynamo A–Z*. The hour-long show would highlight his 26 most amazing tricks from the *Dynamo: Magician Impossible* seasons. Dynamo toured and did various live shows as well. Traveling to different countries being a large part of what made him so diverse.

Dynamo also released various biographies, most of them revolving around his life and lifestyle. However, in 2013 he released a book titled *Nothing Is Impossible: My Story*. Which reached gold status and was named the *Sunday Times* bestseller. The book describes the way Frayne had grown up and how he came from a bad background, and how he could overcome those circumstances.

Four years later in 2017, Dynamo released a beginners guide to magic, titled *Dynamo: The Book of Secrets*. In the book he broke down the most basic tricks and illusions he had done, including step-by-step instructions, as well as including his secrets on how to become a successful performer. The book was aimed at beginners but found itself in the number one position of the *Guardian's* Paperback Nonfiction chart after release.

Frayne was also a part of various charity events and worked alongside various organizations, including the BBC's *Children in Need, Comic Relief and Sport Relief*, and *Theirworld*.

He also worked alongside the United Nations to help Syrian refugees. He is an avid supporter of children's charity programs, knowing what it is like to be bullied and struggling when a child. Frayne did not have the best of childhoods but he grew up to be an honorable man, intent on making a great future for himself and his partner.

He has received various awards and honors throughout his career, receiving praise for his skills as well as his commitment towards making Bradford better for the children who live there now.

ILLUSIONS

In this chapter, the illusions that were created by some of the magicians in the previous chapter will be looked at, examining how they used these illusions and how they differ from the originals.

James Randi

James Randi was known as a skeptic, someone who spent his career trying to prove that no entertainer had some sort of paranormal or spiritual power that helped them create their illusion or show.

One of his most well-known contributions as a performer was the One Million Dollar Paranormal Challenge. To preface the challenge, Randi had started a foundation called the James Randi Education Foundation, as a way to educate people about magicians and illusionists as a way to not get scammed and tricked. Randi and the foundation offered a $1,000,000 prize for anyone who would be able to prove, under scrutiny of scientific testing, that they have supernatural powers.

The foundation was founded in 1996, and Randi was the first to donate $1,000 for the cause, stating that anyone who could prove they had supernatural powers would be able to win the prize money. The prize money of course grew the longer the foundation carried on.

Of course the foundation had set up strict rules that had to be adhered to and while many tried to get the million dollars, very few made it past the initial stages. Randi, however, refused to allow participants to partake if their testing would result in serious injury or death.

However, the rules and regulations changed in 2007. The rules now stated that anyone who wanted to apply needed to have national media recognition, as well as some sort of educational backing, to stop people from wasting time and resources.

A month before the rule changes, television host Larry King challenged a well-known medium, Sylvia Browne, to take the test. Sylvia agreed but in September, approximately 6 months later, Randi appeared on the *Larry King Show* and said that Sylvia had not taken up the challenge at all, refusing to be tested by scientists. However, Sylvia again said she would take the test. In response to this, Randi added a time counter to their website, counting the weeks since Sylvia had said she would take the challenge. Unfortunately, Sylvia never took the test and the counter was ultimately taken down in 2013, after Browne's death.

In June of 2001, Randi and another well-known medium, Rosemary Altea, appeared on the *Larry King Show*. Randi had challenged Rosemary to take the test but she refused to respond, only stating that everyone knew there were various people pretending to be mediums but that those people were lying and fraudsters. The same occurrence happened in 2007 when Randi and Rosemary were on the show again. Randi invited her to take the test but Rosemary ultimately ignored the comment and never took the test.

October 2008 marked a strange year for the foundation and Randi. He had asked the British businessman, Jim McCormick, the inventor of the ADE 651 bomb detector, to take the test after stating that the device was useless and fraudulent. McCormick, however, did not respond to the challenge. McCormick was convicted of three counts of fraud and sentenced to 10 years in prison after it was found that the ADE 651 was indeed useless and hundreds of civilians had lost their lives because of it.

There is a public log of all the participants who have taken part in the million dollar challenge, but the challenge was subsequently shut down when Randi retired from the foundation in 2015.

David Blaine

David Blaine was one of the first few illusionists and card magic creators who filmed most of his interactions. He dabbled in wonderful and mind-boggling tricks and stunts.

Buried Alive

April 5, 1999 marked the day that Blaine was placed in a plastic box, underneath a tank filled with 3 tons of water, for 7 days. His only method of communication was a buzzer that Blaine could use to be able to let emergency staff know if he needed help.

According to various sources, there was only 6 inches of headroom and two inches of room around the sides for any movement. During the stunt about 75 000 people were at the site, and on the final day various preparations had to be made to help Blaine exit the area without getting hurt.

A group of workers had to remove 75 cubic feet of sand that surrounded the coffin before a crane was used to remove the tank from the top of the coffin; thereafter Blaine emerged from the coffin.

Frozen in Time

In November of 2000 Blaine did one of his most dangerous stunts. In Time Square, New York City, he would stand inside ice for 72 hours. The show was captured and aired as a television special. Blaine was scantily dressed and seemed to be cold before he had even stepped into the area. Blaine stood on a platform, purely to show that he was indeed standing inside the ice block.

Ice was stacked around him. There was a tube for air and water, as well as any other bodily needs. After 63 hours and 42 minutes, Blaine was removed by emergency medical staff who feared that his body might be going into shock. He was rushed to the closest hospital and Blaine stated to several news outlets in an interview that his recovery from the stunt took almost a month and he would not be attempting it again, as it was far too dangerous.

In 2010 Blaine's record was broken by Hezi Dean in Israel, when he was encased for a whopping 66 hours.

Vertigo

May 2002 marked the stunt that seemed to be the easiest but also somewhat more dangerous than the ones before. Blaine was lifted 100 feet into the air, onto a 22 inch pillar in Bryant Park in New York.

Blaine was not harnessed or strapped to the pillar but handles had been added for him to hold on to in case the weather were to become somewhat turbulent. Blaine was able to stay on the pillar for 35 hours, after which he jumped to a makeshift platform that had been constructed out of cardboard boxes. While he had no severe injuries, he did suffer from a mild concussion.

In his 2009 TED Talk, Blaine explained that the worst hours were the last as he started hallucinating, making the stunt more dangerous than at the beginning.

Above the Below

This stunt, like the others, was dangerous, but Blaine wanted to test his endurance. In 2003 Blaine was encapsulated inside a transparent plexiglass box. The box was 3 feet by 3 feet by 3 feet, allowing limited space for movement. The box was suspended 30 feet in the air to the south of the River Thames, in London.

A webcam had been installed so that people could watch and see how the progress went. This particular stunt lasted for 44 days and during this time Blaine consumed 1.2 gallons of water per day but he never consumed any food.

Various news outlets wrote articles and interviews regarding this, even the then president George W. Bush commenting on it. During this time, various people attacked the box, throwing food and other objects at the box. A man had also been arrested for trying to tamper with the tubing that would give Blaine water.

The *BBC News* had a doctor confirm that Blaine's change in taste in the later days was caused by ketones being burned by the body when it starts going into the starvation phase.

What few knew about this stunt was that while the stunt itself was dangerous, his recovery was even worse. Once Blaine emerged he was rushed to a nearby hospital. He had lost 25% of his body weight. The biggest concern was the refeeding process as he would not be able to eat normally. In the end Blaine suffered from hypophosphatemia (an instance where there are low levels of phosphorus in your blood) and fluid retention, both of these most commonly known to be a part of refeeding syndrome.

Drowned Alive

David Blaine started performing his Drowned Alive stunt in 2006. This stunt lasted 7 days and the first time he did it was on May 1st, in front of the Lincoln Center in New York City.

J.M. Luijt at Dutch Wikipedia, CC BY 2.5 NL, via
Wikimedia Commons

He was submerged into a water tank that was spherical, and had an 8 foot diameter. The sphere was filled with isotonic saline. Blaine suffered liver and kidney damage due to the stunt. Once he had completed it Blaine had gone into an agreement with Yale University to allow them to monitor him to see how prolonged submersion would be on human psychological levels.

Revolution

This was one of Blaine's most interesting stunts. In November of 2006, Blaine was cuffed to a gyroscope that would be rotating the entire time.

The goal was for him to stay without food and water and escape within 16 hours. Unfortunately, it took Blaine a little longer and he only freed himself after 52 hours.

Blaine had various other stunts that he performed, some for which he was criticized while others were wildly loved. Most of them encapsulate both the thrilling feeling and the anxiety and danger of something horrible going wrong.

Criss Angel

Criss Angel was one of the magicians who revolutionized magic and how we see it today; he was one of the first to bring back big and dangerous shows, using his showmanship to create large-scale shows that astounded anyone, no matter their level of enjoyment when it came to magic.

While he had various shows and television series where one could see his acts, there is one that stood out among all of his stunts and shows.

Water Torture Cell

Similar to the stunt Houdini had performed, Angel decided to try the Chinese Torture Cell stunt. He had been practicing the stunt in a neighbor's pool next to his mother's house; unfortunately, he had only been able to stay under water for 12 consecutive hours.

The 24 hours before the performance, Angel went without food and water, wanting to make sure that he did not need to use the bathroom while he was part of the stunt. The stunt was performed near the WWE entertainment store that is situated in Time Square, New York.

During the entirety of the stunt, Angel went through 16 oxygen tanks. As part of his stunt, Angel had to remove his shackles and cuffs by himself once he emerged from the tank. The tank, a similar size as a phone booth, with a capacity of 220 US-gallons, had a pipe that allowed Angel access to the oxygen tanks.

When Angel was ready to emerge, he pulled the oxygen pipe away and assistants of his closed black curtains around the box, keeping the view of his escape obscured. Once he had finished the stunt and had successfully escaped, he was taken to a nearby hospital and treated for severe dehydration. Angel also commented on the experience he had, mentioning that he was semi-conscious, had jaw-fatigue, and suffered from overheating.

Penn & Teller

Penn & Teller are a great duo and the tricks and illusions include a lot of pranks and clever behind-the-scenes details that would roll over into political satire. The two use their methods to weed out frauds and expose them to the world. They employ some intense violence and the shock appeal that comes with it to put their point across, making sure to always create a comedic undertone to their shows.

While their tricks were often prefaced as a "trick gone bad" show, they did add some sense of danger and realism to their shows, making sure that while the subject matter could be hard to swallow or difficult to understand, there would always be some sort of comedic relief for the audience, to make the subject matter seem less intense and palatable.

What Penn & Teller often did was to expose a trick on purpose, showing the audience exactly how the trick was constructed and how it would play out. They would do this far more spectacularly than just explaining how the trick would be, making it more of an experience than just an exposition of the trick. What made Penn & Teller one of the most interesting acts was that even though they exposed other magicians' tricks, they did it in such a way that while the audience understood that the trick was being exposed, they still felt like something magical was happening.

One of the most popular examples of this was when Penn & Teller did the show *Off the Deep End*. In the specific trick, Teller was locked inside a wooden crate and then placed in shark-infested waters. The live audience of course only saw that Teller entered the crate and was now in shark-infested waters, while the television audience saw a clip where Teller had escaped through a trap door before the box was moved to the water, and he was sitting and enjoying a snack while he waited for his cue.

The two often performed popular tricks like this, exposing the trick but making it a fun experience for the audience to enjoy: tricks like the bullet-catching trick as well as the sawing a woman in half stunt. While they used satire to expose certain tricks, they would often also use their tricks to discuss difficult topics, creating awareness on certain issues.

This can be found in their politically charged tricks. For example, the duo performs a trick where the United States flag disappears. The disappearance was made by wrapping the flag in the United States Bill of Rights and then setting the flag on fire. In the end it would mean that the flag has disappeared but the Bill of Rights remains. The trick would usually end where the flag would reappear where it was on the flagpole.

Another trick that became popular with their audience was the concept that endangering those on stage with you makes the audience culprits, and a part of unnecessary risk, and puts more than just your partner in danger. They would explain this by having a nail gun on stage. Penn would start by firing a bunch of nails into a board and then turning the nail gun to his hand, never once hitting his hand.

The pace would quicken and he would go from shooting nails into a board and then turning the gun towards his hand, then he turned

the gun to Teller's crotch and a blank would fire. Before the trick
would end they would explain why involving the audience in a
simple trick like that would make them complicit in unnecessary risk
towards each other.

MODERN DAY MAGIC

When locking at the vast difference between the magicians that have been covered in Chapter 2, and their tricks in Chapter 3, and then comparing them to the magicians in Chapter 4 and their tricks and stunts covered in the previous chapter, it feels as if modern day magic strayed away from doing the same tricks over and over to something far more daring. Magic has turned from sleight of hand to pushing yourself to the extreme, seeing how far you can push your mental and physical health all for the sake of magic. They wanted to create something unique and wonderful, something that would be loved by all, no matter their level of interest in magic.

What is even more interesting is the fact that magicians went from over-the-top shows and large events to sleight-of-hand tricks, where the devil is in the details. Many of the modern magicians we know now do not do wild and amazing tricks, but rather stick to sleight-of-hand tricks where the audience is so focused on what the card trick will be that they completely miss the small details that lead to solving the puzzle.

What makes modern day magic so interesting is the fact that magic now has to evolve with technology. In the early 1900s and even in the late 19o0s, technology was used but not as much, because technology was not as easily accessible as it is now.

One reason why modern magicians can return back to magical roots and create daring and extraordinary stunts and illusions that could endanger them is because the resources they would need are so much easier to access. This also means that the technology used to create the stunts or illusions in today's day and age are planned to such detail and intensity that they have escape and exit plans for each and every type of scenario that could happen.

To explain the difference that modern technology can make, let's take a look at the film *Now You See Me*. The film was released in 2013, with a great cast, including Morgan Freeman, Isla Fisher,

Woody Harrelson, Jesse Eisenberg, Mark Ruffalo, and Dave Franco. The film was categorized as a heist thriller but it resonated more with those who had a passion and love for magic.

This is one of the most popular films surrounding magic, although the second installment has been shot down by various reviewers as something that is not exactly filled with magic but rather just a show of lights and spectacle. Fortunately for us, the first film shows us what magic in the modern times are like. They take basic tricks and illusions and throughout the time that the film is running they explain how the trick or illusion played out. Oftentimes it will be as a flashback, while one of the characters narrates the entire way through, or it will simply show a small cutscene, similar to how Penn & Teller would show the television audience a different clip than what the live audience sees.

You will somehow be a part of the illusion in some instances, being included in the trick, the fourth wall in film being broken to explain how exactly they had been able to do the certain trick or stunt.

This brings into question the capacity that one has to use technology alongside magic and how important technology could be to make magic something even more entertaining or extravagant. One of the most important things to consider here is the fact that our technological advances are moving so quickly that some parts of our everyday lives are barely able to keep up. What about magic then? In the next section, we will consider the impact technology has had on magic and how it has changed our views on what magic can and has done.

Modern Magic and Technology

What makes technology a great addition to magic is the fact that you can now make stunts far more dangerous and exciting. You can add in subtle illusions and sleight of hand that would otherwise be far more difficult. However, what we seem to be forgetting is that the moment we add technology to something that is so detail-oriented and detail-specific is the fact that it very quickly becomes the norm for anything related to such tricks or illusions, taking us further away from the simpler more basic roots of magic, such as the magician's skill in sleight of hand or close-up magic.

When science fiction author Arthur C. Clarke created his three laws for human advancement, little did he know that those laws would not only affect science fiction, but the entire way we perceive and view advancement when it comes to technology and magic.

Clarke's first law stated that if a scientist says that something was possible, he was certainly right, and if the same scientist stated that something was impossible then he was probably correct as well. This creates the concept that when a magician says that he can levitate he is probably right and when he says that he cannot levitate he is also probably correct. This causes problems, not only for the audience members but also for the magician themselves. How can levitation happen if it is acknowledged to be impossible by the magician himself?

The first law dictates that with or without technology anything is possible, and while the statement may seem valid and true, it is without a doubt something that needs to be considered when using technological advancement when it comes to magic. Using technology alongside magic makes the possibilities even more endless than doing magic without technology. Anything is possible without technology but technology makes the things that were considered impossible in the 1900s possible in 2022.

Clark's second law states the only way that one can actually test and know the limits of what is actually possible, is to actually venture into the impossible and to test the limitations of those scenarios.

This means that to be able to prove or disprove the possibility of something, you would have to consider the impossibility of it and test the boundaries surrounding it. This law can clearly be seen when magicians attempt to do tricks that seem impossible (ie, levitation), and then prove them possible. It is one of the most common rules that can be applied to absolutely everything in our everyday lives: As Henry Ford once said, "Whether you think you can or you think you can't, you are right."

The third and final law that Clarke created was absolutely the most important when it comes to magic and the magical realm. The third law states that if technology was sufficiently advanced, it would be difficult to distinguish it from magic. This law is extremely difficult to comprehend in terms of magic, as the line between technology and magic becomes blurred.

When considering Arthur C. Clarke's third law, that sufficient enough technology will be indistinguishable from magic, you can really see the battle that this becomes. Commonly magic is considered to be something that is supposed to be unexplainable, and while for some it may be something easy to comprehend, for others it would be something that is fascinating and wonderous. Modern times make it so that everyone in the audience understands that there is trickery involved, and it falls to the magician to make sure that his work is undetected. Consider the stark contrast this casts to the early 1600s, where this approach and understanding was not something common at all.

The blurred line between magic and technology makes for interesting viewing but it also leads one to believe that magic cannot exist without the touch and help of technology. It is difficult to use this as a basic way of viewing magic, as magic can stand on its own, and it has, but technology has become such an integral part of magic and how the world has been perceiving it, that it is difficult to imagine magic without the interference and help of technology.

This might be why so many modern magicians either choose to go back to the roots of magic, or they choose to expose other magicians for being fraudulent. Technology has changed the way magic grows and expands, all over the world.

If we consider for the moment that technology is evolving and growing at a rapid pace, and magic is growing with it, we can assume that there will be a place and time where what is considered magic to be the norm, and will become something that is far less magical and much more commonplace. It will be something that we see every day and do not bat an eye at for seeing, similar to how we now have artificial intelligence, like Siri and the Google Assistant that can book meetings and appointments for you.

What you need to consider then, is the fact that magic was a way to explain the unexplainable. While magic was a convenient way to deal with new things, especially in the early 1900s, it has changed vastly from what it was to what it is now. It is important to note these changes, to be aware of all the differences, whether they are subtle or not.

What we tend to forget is the fact that our way of approaching both science and technology is fundamentally the same way we approached magic in the old days. We used to test and prod and ask questions, and wander into the unknown of what it could be and what it could become, that magic and technology could be considered the exact same thing. Magic might be something we struggle to understand, but once we ask the right questions and push boundaries, we start to see how things are pieced together and how things are created, which is essentially the scientific approach.

However, while we still wander beyond our boundaries, there are some who believe we do so purely out of necessity, making technological advancement something that is far more monetary related than doing so out of pure curiosity and wonder.

Consider the influence magic has on mythology and fables that we know today. So many of the myths we've heard have created the illusion that there was some magical string of fate or larger-than-life cosmos that kept everything in sync and together, and humans accepted this as a common explanation. Those in power used misinformation and lack of education as a way to keep themselves in power. This meant that it was in the common folks best interest to stay misinformed, as questioning or going against those in power could often lead to their death. Thus, 'magic' and 'the supernatural' were accepted explanations for the unexplainable.

Magic was such a common occurrence that people even used it as part of rituals and traditions. Ritual and traditional magic was however something that was highly revered. People who became spiritual leaders or healers had status and what they knew became something 'secret,' one had to be part of a select group who were privy to this type of information. Magic became an integral part of who certain people were and what they stood for.

Take for instance Egyptian culture, where High Priests were sent to perform magical rituals for births or funerals, or similarly the Greeks, who used a mixture of medicinal practice and magical healing enchantments to be able to send the dead on to the right realm. This gave people the power to be able to confront the unknown of death or what the future may hold.

Consider the times we are in now. We constantly have the entire internet at our fingertips. We walk around with a device only a few inches bigger than the palm of our hands that can call someone in a different country, or find information from a library we did not even know existed. Would that not be considered to be something magical?

To be frank, our level of curiosity has become nothing more than scientific pursuits. There are no longer people who do magic for the sake of it; there is no longer a fear of the unknown. We have access to millions of resources in a matter of seconds and the little bit of fear that is left can be placated by a video on YouTube of a kitten rolling around with a ball of string.

What is interesting to note, however, is the fact that our easy access to science and information has led us down the same path that our ancestors were on. We have come to a place where we see magic the same way they did, but we can only know this by looking back to how the experience was shaped. Many explain magic as an experience that has only been 'viewed' differently.

Consider this scenario: take someone from the 1920s and hand them an iPhone. They will not know what on earth this device is and if you were to explain to them the power that the small item holds they would most certainly laugh and tell you that it is not possible. How could such a small item hold the world's knowledge and still be small enough to fit in your pocket? They would believe it to be some form of witchcraft, or magic, something evil perhaps. Now consider yourself at a younger age: consider how you grew up with technology and how this seems to be the norm for you. The device is still magical in its roots. It is still something that can be seen as magical because it still does the most amazing things, the only difference being that you have grown up with this item, you have become so accustomed to what it can do that it has become the norm, and the moment you can no longer use it for its intended purposes you would become annoyed or angry even.

What makes the technological influence somewhat unexplainable at times is the fact that even though you can have all the information regarding a scenario, and you have all the possible paths planned out, there is still a fraction of information that is unattainable. Something could always go wrong. Something could break, something could dislodge or not happen the way it is supposed to, and that would certainly hinder the results of the stunt or scientific experiment. The same could be said about magic, whether watching a stunt by Harry Houdini or David Blaine.

Technology Influence

Take the sleight-of-hand artist Dynamo. He is commonly known as a sleight-of-hand and card illusionist. It has become so common for him to be doing these kinds of tricks that some people don't even show interest in his tricks anymore. While he still does old-school magic and sleight-of-hand illusions, it has become the norm for people to see some sort of magician like this in the streets or in restaurants, that the sense of wonder and excitement has somewhat diminished.

For younger generations, however, one can argue that old-school magic would be something far more interesting, as the level of danger and strain it took would seem otherworldly for them. The question is, however: Do they actually realize that the magicians like Harry Houdini and John Henry Maskelyne were risking their lives for tricks and illusions that had no certain outcome? Or do they just assume that the technology we have now is something that was available back then as well?

The rate at which technology is growing and evolving is slowly leaving magic and so many other fields behind because it is becoming commonplace for creators and entertainers to be the best at their craft in an ever-changing world. We have come to a space where you have to be the best of the best of the best to get an inch of recognition.

What technology has also done is to put more people at risk. We see more and more riskier performances, amateurs performing tricks on skyscrapers with only the bare minimum when it comes to safety regulation, purely because technology has allowed anyone who can do basic magic to put it out into the world. This just means that people who are truly talented and want to get recognized are putting themselves and their audience at risk by doing stunts and illusions that are that much more dangerous.

Consider magicians like David Blaine and Criss Angel, who would push their mental and physical health to the limits for their audience. They would endanger themselves purely to be able to say that they had survived, no matter how bad it ended up hurting their bodies.

Technology has for sure revolutionized the way we see things and the way we interact with the world, but considering the gap it has created between modern magicians and the old-school magicians, we cannot help but wonder if this was truly what we had hoped for. Technology has definitely revolutionized the way that we see magic, and while there are only subtle differences between the two, we can still surmise that science and magic exist on the same plane: The only way for us to be able to ascertain the truth, whether it is scientific, technological, or magical is by venturing into the unknown.

Magic Today, Reality Tomorrow

One of the most important things we need to remember in our day and age is the fact that, along with technology growing so fast, there comes a point where the magic we perform today becomes an integral part of what the future may need, and it may become reality tomorrow.

Referring back to the film *Now You See Me*, there are various magic tricks that are shown that are at their root old-school tricks, but alongside the newer technological advancements that we have seen become a trend, become something of the norm.

Now You See Me Explained

One of the best ways to drive home exactly how technology has influenced both old-school magic and newer magic is to look at examples found in the film *Now You See Me*. Being able to link the technology to the magic trick and seeing how technology can and has changed the field will allow us a better view of what will become the norm in terms of magic and its technological future.

To explain how the tricks were mastered and how they translated from old-school trickery to modern times, the following section will delve into how the tricks were explained throughout the film *Now You See Me*.

It is important to note that the film starts off explaining the different backstories from each of the main characters, each of them being a street performer and illusionist. What makes the film a great way to explain modern influences on magic is the fact that they often give glimpses behind the scenes to explain the truth behind each trick. While the viewer would only be able to tell this once the trick has been finalized, it was an important way to connect with viewers.

What makes *Now You See Me* such a good film is the fact that it brought magic and illusion and the skills you need to be able to perform sufficiently into the spotlight, and magic and its popularity rose quite significantly. While the bigger more elaborate tricks and illusions were explained, there are smaller and more basic tricks that were left unexplained by the director and producer, adding the touch of magic and mystery that one would like to see in films surrounding magic. There are quite a few tricks that were not discussed within the film, and in this section—by covering the trick and how it was influenced and changed due to modern influences with technology—allows us to see exactly how well technology does when it comes to measuring up against magic.

Handcuff

Of all the various tricks and illusions that can be found within the entirety of the film, this is one of the most fun ones to talk about. This is one of the few tricks that was created in the film that actually did not need any extra editing or superimposition to be able to set the scene up or complete the trick.

In the scene our main character is being interrogated and his wrists are cuffed together. Once the interrogating officer leans into our main character, he shifts, and seconds later the cuffs are wrapped around the officer's wrists.

While it seems like there had to be some form of digital changes or enhancing for this trick, there was none. If you looked at the way Danny (the main character) was sitting, you could see that he had already picked the lock for the handcuffs and the moment the inter-rogating officer was in his face he purely had to flick the cuffs around in a quick manner and the cuffs locked themselves.

This is a perfect example of how modern technology has changed magic but magic can still stand on its own. The scene looked intense and left viewers in shock, but the sleight of hand and focus on the intense interaction between the two characters created for the perfect illusion.

Piranha Tank

While this remains one of the most intense tricks in the film, partly due to the fact that the props had gotten stuck and the actress had almost drowned, it was amazing seeing one of the most popular tricks of the late 1800s and early 1900s be used in the film.

The trick was similar to the water torture cell, the only difference being the fact that there were piranha in the water. Fortunately for the actress, and all of us, they were 100% pure CGI. This makes the trick even more magical in my opinion. Technology had evolved so much so that the audience is left with a panging fear in their chest that someone had just died.

The scene in the film starts with the actress Isla Lang Fisher (Henley Reeves) being lowered into the tank, and then being absolutely obliterated by the fish, only for her to emerge unharmed a few seconds later, from elsewhere in the scene. This was extremely magical and while we now know that half of the scene was CGI, we are still left with a sense of wonder, knowing that something similar could not be recreated in real life as it would be far too dangerous.

Bubble Trick

The magician that was consulting on the film was responsible for the conceptualization of this trick and, honestly, it is one of the fan favorites.

The four horsemen (the four main characters) appear to be hosting their first show. They create large bubbles, filling the theater, and once one of them is big enough, one of the horsemen jumps into the bubble and floats around the room.

Of course, levitation has been practiced and shown for millennia, and various magicians have portrayed their version of it. However, most magicians would do so near the stage, where any wiring and tools could not be seen.

However, modern technology made it easier for them to recreate the floating bubble scene as something that has never before been seen. They wanted to portray something that real-world magicians and illusionists had never before been able to do, and honestly, without the help of modern technology. there is little to prove that it would have been able to be done.

The production team opted to use ample amounts of wiring to be able to create the perfect scene here. The wiring, along with some after editing to create the bubbles, made for an amazing scene.

Deadly Plastic Card

One of the most action-packed scenes that could be found in the film is when one of the horsemen encounters the FBI agent, who has been chasing them, inside their apartment.

During their encounter, instead of picking up a weapon that could actually hurt the agent, Dave (the fourth horsemen) opts to use his deck of cards to fight the officer. At first the FBI agent is confused, right until Dave throws the first card, and it slashes his cheek.

What makes this trick so amazing is the fact that cards can and have been able to be thrown with such accuracy that they can cut certain items, even human flesh. The actor practiced as much as he could and it is said that he did in fact cut the actor who was playing the FBI agent multiple times.

It is amazing to see the difference between tricks that need technology to become more than just fantasy (like the bubble trick) and those that are so rooted in science and skill that they are anything but magic.

Key in the Soda

When looking back at the scene where Danny is being interrogated, Danny suggests that the officer who is interrogating him turn around their soda can. As they do, the key along with the soda tumbles out of the can and onto the table.

This trick is commonly performed by street artists, and one of the most common ways to do this is to subtly slip the coin or object into the can when you are opening it. There is also another method that is used less often, where a small cut would be made into the can and the object would be added into the can before sealing the cut back up.

However, since neither of these two methods were used during the scene, we can ascertain that the editing department did their jobs to the finest detail, adding the correct amount of 'magic' to the scene and letting the key fall from inside the can.

Modern Magic and Social Media

What makes modern magic so entertaining is the fact that even as we continue to support and nourish traditional magic. We also have more and more entertainers who are delving deep into learning the old-school tricks and illusions. They are using modern technology to revolutionize and change those skills to be captured as entertainment for a modern viewership.

Entertainers are forced to work on a modern platform in fear of being left behind. And while the statement may seem a little rough and intense in terms of an ever-changing world, most feel that you either sink or swim in the magic business. Being able to stand out above the rest of those surrounding will only help you in the long run.

In no way, shape, or form is it bad to include modern technology and modern skills into magic, nor is it bad to stick to older, more traditional skills and illusions. It is merely something that is ever changing. alongside technology, and being able to actually grow with both technology and the way that it influences magic will make for an even better performance.

What is important to note is the fact that social media has also been influenced by magic. When thinking of your phone and the world and wealth of information that it holds, we cannot for a moment fathom that what we hold in our hands are magical. As mentioned before, we have grown up with this; we have grown up with the internet and access to certain things whenever we need to have access to it.

This access would only be possible because someone believed enough in the unknown and their idea of what the future could be like to start working towards this goal. Hour upon hour of research and questions have gone into creating the perfect little handheld device for everyone, and we still get newer versions every day.

Considering that we are an ever-changing human race, constantly on the brink of discovering something new or looking for something bigger and better, it is safe to assume that as with science, magic will never truly leave or disappear, aspects of it will simply turn into the norm for us. Weird things like holographics and floating around will become the normal thing and everything else will become old school and traditional, such as rotary phones and telephone booths!

Technology is amazing and at the rate that it is evolving it is astounding to see the changes we are making. What should, however, be taken into question is the fact that somewhere we as humans might not be able to keep up with ever-changing technology, or that the resources required to do so will no longer be available, and if we do not have an answer to that question now, will we have one in the future?

Magic and Science

Magic has grown quite considerably in the last few decades. It has become popular and you see more and more pop culture surrounding magic. It has become so important in the scientific community that Ronald A Rensink and Gustav Kuhn, both psychologists and great in their field, have posited that the technological advancement and the impact it has had on magic has allowed us ways to be able to use magic in the field of psychology.

The two psychologists have been backed by several others, but one of their most prominent opposers has been Peter Lamont. He used his article "Problems with the mapping of magic tricks" to counter Rensink and Kuhn's position that magic can be used to better psychology. Magic has not only had an impact on technology but also on how we live our modern lives, and how our future will play out, even if it does not seem that way in the beginning.

With the resurgence of magic and the concepts along with it, there has been a vast and largely growing wave of studies surrounding magic. It also looks at how magic can be scientifically used and developed for certain skills and how certain types of magic can be utilized for the human race, and its future. Rensink and Kuhn (2015) posit that magic needs its own science, and they have had various others counter their argument for this, but it seems like the resurgence in magic and what it can do might be far more viable than we think.

There has been a lot of research and study surrounding magic, and how it has played various roles in our everyday life, as well as how it impacts our belief systems and points of view. This resurgence of study surrounding magic has prompted various scientists and researchers to come to the point where suggestions surrounding a 'science' for magic should be adopted. This specific field of study would test and research the human mind and body when one comes across something magical and completely 'impossible.'

Rensink and Kuhn have suggested a dedicated framework to be able to create such a science and how it will be utilized. The framework would need to be split into three different sets of issues that might arise. The first set would be the entities or individuals who would be relevant to the specific study or event; the second set would be the questions that can be asked surrounding the individuals or entities, as well as the event; and the final set would be the answers that would be derived from the entities, individuals, and the event itself.

Considering how magic is structured, the sets would be defined in the following ways, (keep in mind that each set would focus on magic itself). The first set would encompass the nature of the experience, how magical the experience would be. The second set would be looked at in terms of how each individual trick or illusion would be able to create the magical experience found in set one; and the final set would be to create an organized database of the known tricks in a comprehensive and detailed way. This framework would also include a level that would focus on how to use various methods of magic as tools for investigating and bettering other fields of study.

Lamont had countered Rensink and Kuhn's argument, stating that although the base level they had suggested might work, they will be unable to accurately study magic tricks and how they affect people, as there is little to no structure when it comes to these specific tricks. Lamont used this reasoning as a way to say that the *science of magic* will never truly be successful. Rensink and Kuhn countered that even though this would create more challenges for them, it did not negate the capacity they have for creating the science nor did it stop the possibility of science for magic to exist. The two even posited that it could positively contribute to studying the mind more successfully.

Rensink and Kuhn mentioned that the tricks Lamont had mentioned in his counter-argument did exist. And that though there were a large variety of tricks, the science of magic would not focus on the different types of tricks, but would rather focus on the *effect* those tricks have. They use an example to explain their point, stating that the first level of their framework would focus on what makes the magical experience unique. They would, for instance, look at the different types of wonder one can have for a certain type of magical transformation or trick.

What they also point out is how objective magic really is, and how different people have different impressions of what magical items are. They note that it is important to remember that what is actually irrelevant here, is how exactly the experience is creating a feeling of wonder. They phrase it in the following way: "the scientific study of magic is not concerned with the nature of magic tricks themselves, but with the *magical aspects of experience created by these tricks*" (Rensink & Kuhn, 2015).

They posit that magic tricks are of course important but not on the first level; this only becomes a truth on the second level. The second level of the framework focuses on how the effects that are created in each individual *are* created. What is important to remember here is the fact that each trick is a complex thing and they are commonly known to have multiple complex parts that work together seamlessly to create a successful trick. What Rensink and Kuhn propose is that each trick has a set of rules that the magician follows to ensure success of the trick, making sure that whatever happens, the trick does not fail. They use the example of misdirection, indicating that one small movement or a simple sound that distracts the audience members enough will allow the magician to continue his trick without the audience member noticing his misdirection or sleight of hand.

Rensink and Khun posit that knowing the smaller details of each trick will slowly but surely allow them to deeply understand how each individual trick works. In other words, the better they know each individual component, the easier it will be to piece the components together and understand a trick in its entirety.

The two counter Lamont's point further by stating that they understand why he suggests that magic tricks have a lacking structure to them, but while each trick does have an endless 'variety' of items that can be used alongside, and that there are endless variations of speech patterns that can be used, there are methods around these two issues. They offer that phrase-structure grammar could be used to analyze the different structures, and if that perhaps did not work, they also suggest something like psycho-linguistic experimentation.

Rensink and Kuhn suggest that the correct selection of methods of study for the basic elements will make it easier to understand, even if there are infinite possibilities. Magic is known to have different components and some of the same components are used in different tricks. Lamont states that the same components are used for different tricks, and states that the ambiguity here may cause a problem. Rensink and Kuhn posit that there will be no issues with the different components if they are creating functional replacements. In other words, if the same components are used for different tricks, it is perfectly okay, because the same components are used out of function, not create extra steps for no apparent reason.

Lamont also states that the vast variety will only get worse because there are no boundaries that have been set by the two. The change in timing, effect, or how a card appears will cause it to be classified as a different variety of a specific trick. Rensink and Kuhn counter this argument by stating that they have considered this possibility and while they know that this might happen, they know that it has not stopped other fields of science from continuing their studies. They use the example of different animals, stating that while animals are different and they change constantly, it has not placed any impeding forces on biology. They offer a simple solution of using abstraction methods to be able to counter the variety problem.

Lamont also mentions the different contingency methods that need to be taken into account, and again Rensink and Kuhn have a response for his concerns. They suggest grouping together different tricks that have the same types of effects on the audience. They also discuss another method, where they would define a trick depending on the method it uses; this method would allow them to just purely explain the use of the trick based on what the performance would be.

They do, however, suggest that the choice they make for methodology would be dependent on a variety of factors, such as the other tricks that are used during the performance, the overall feeling of the audience, and how the magician would be feeling at that exact moment. They posit that the contingency here reflects the essence of the artistry behind magic, but it does not exclude the capacity to scientifically study the magic trick.

They note that people respond to similar situations in similar ways; there will always be some sort of stable element. In other words, no matter their method of study, they will find the correct context because of the stable regularity that is human reactions. If this statement were not true, magic would not have become popular at all, as only a few people would have enjoyed it while the masses would have ignored or detested it. This also means that the regularities (the way that people react the same way to the same stimulus) can be studied in a systematic method.

The highest level of their framework, commonly known as 'the systemization level,' is critiqued by Lamont, stating that the lack of structure from tricks would keep them from classifying the tricks in a structured way. Rensink and Kuhn note here that the systemic level of their framework is only the first level, and that even if they could not create a classification system, the rest of their framework would still stand.

Rensink and Kuhn state that they had never said or posited that they needed to be able to classify and do a complete inventory of each trick, and while it would be a goal that they would want to achieve, it is not necessary for their framework as their system will still hold value even if it is incomplete.

One of the most interesting questions that comes up when thinking of this is the fact that even if they could categorize and put all the tricks into an inventory, how would they do this? Generally, in such systems, scientists would use natural classification, letting the natural elements of an item define the categories. But how would one do so when it comes to even the specific singular elements of a trick?

Rensink and Kuhn state that natural classification is not something that would be necessary for this specific framework. They suggest that "It is entirely possible, for example, to relate in a systematic way designs described by continuous parameters, even when these parameters interact with each other in complex ways" (Rensink & Kuhn, 2015).

The suggestion is this then: that a classification system for magic tricks will be a complex problem that will include vast amounts of empirical details. They suggest that their papers on the topic are on some level just their practice for the philosophy of what magic is. They continue the article by explaining that they have a different method of misdirection classification, using only two principles for their system.

The first principle is that they should use as many psychological mechanisms as they possibly can, and the second principle is to have the taxonomy focus on the mechanisms that are affected and not the mechanisms that control the tricks. By using these principles, they will greatly change the number of random decisions that will create a large collection of magic tricks.

Both Rensink and Kuhn agree that there might be other classification systems out there and that those systems might even be better than their own, stating that even a science like biology has different types of taxonomy. They believe that finding the right classification system will take time and they believe deeply that it can be done, they just need to find the perfect way to do so, and doing so will help not only them but others as well.

Rensink and Kuhn thus want their research and studying to be able to help other scientific fields to be able to better understand various parts of the brain, and how it creates perceptions of items or people, how memory and reasoning work, and how these aspects are activated and used in different instances. They posit that it might also help them and others to better understand magic.

Considering all of the above information, and the history that magic has, it is important to note that scientific advancements, when it comes to research, are just as important to magic as they are to technology.

Considering the impact that this research could have on magic and even other scientific studies makes magic only that much more wonderful. It is absolutely amazing to think that something as small as a disappearing coin could revolutionize the way we think about religion and technology or even just the daily hobbies we enjoy.

Take into consideration the recent developments that have been made with regards to music and how the brain reacts to certain music and certain genres of music. It has revolutionized the way that artists create music and the way we listen to music; headphones and earphone creators have changed and adapted their equipment and products to enable us to have a better experience, and YouTube has made it possible for more budding artists to get exposure without having to create demo tapes or find an agent.

What makes this even more amazing is the fact that when the studies surrounding music first began, the same concerns were thrown at scientists' doors. They were bombarded with issues that seemed trivial to those who were willing to change the world, and here we are, years later, the world a better place for it.

CONCLUSION

Whether you consider the older skills and techniques that one must use or the newer modern magic that we have come to know as normal, it is important to remember that as long as the feeling of wonder and mystery remains, there will always be magic.

Magic has come a long way from where it all started. Whether it came from witchcraft and religious rituals or from a sense of curiosity and wonder with regards to all things unknown, it is something that will stick with us for years and years to come. Whether it will still be called 'magic' remains to be seen, however.

Technology has had a very intense impact on what we presume magic is and what magic will be in the next decade, and as mentioned before, what could be something magical and astounding today could very well be something that becomes our reality and 'the norm' in the near distant future. Technology, science, and magic walk hand in hand, all three rooted in human curiosity and what it could be if one were to push the boundaries of what you know and don't know.

Consider perhaps magicians like David Blaine, Dynamo, and Criss Angel. All of them found fame alongside technology, by using modern technology to make their stunts more interesting or terrifying.

Magic has and always will be something that enamors us and makes people wonder. It brings up the concept that there are many wonders beyond what we know and understand, and that is something that needs to be cultivated. Children absolutely adore magic, and while some adults hold on to that sense of wonder, others seem to lose it along the way when they grow up, and honestly, the sense of wonder and curiosity people have is what drives the world to change. It is the one thing that drives and pushes for new things, the need to have something even more amazing than what we already have.

It is important to never lose one's sense of wonder and curiosity, as it is the key to becoming better and more magical, whether we know it or not. We are the only ones who could be holding ourselves back, and magic has a funny way of showing us that even the impossible is possible, if you just go beyond your comfort zone.

One of the most important things to remember when it comes to magic, life, and everything it holds can be summarized by a quote from Albert Einstein during an interview with *LIFE Magazine* in 1955:

> *The important thing is not to stop questioning. Curiosity has its own reason for existence. One cannot help but be in awe when he contemplates the mysteries of eternity, of life, of the marvelous structure of reality. It is enough if one tries merely to comprehend a little of this mystery each day.*

THANKS FOR READING

Dear reader,

Thank you for reading *Famous Magicians in History*.

If you enjoyed this book, please leave a review where you bought it. It helps more than most people think.

Don't forget your FREE book chapters!

You will also be among the first to know of FREE review copies, discount offers, bonus content, and more.

Go to:

https://www.SFNonfictionBooks.com/Free-Chapters

Thanks again for your support.

REFERENCES

American Museum of Magic. (n.d.). *History of Magic*. American Museum of Magic. Retrieved January 25, 2022, http://americanmuseumofmagic.com/history-of-magic/

Chand, N. (2021, August 18). *The magic tricks in Now You See Me explained*. Looper.com. https://www.looper.com/491116/the-magic-tricks-in-now-you-see-me-explained/

Criss Angel. (2022, January 12). Wikipedia. https://en.wikipedia.org/wiki/Criss_Angel

David Blaine. (2022, January 1). Wikipedia. https://en.wikipedia.org/wiki/David_Blaine

Derren Brown. (2022, January 20). Wikipedia. https://en.wikipedia.org/wiki/Derren_Brown

David Copperfield (illusionist). (2022, February 8). Wikipedia. https://en.wikipedia.org/wiki/David_Copperfield_(illusionist)

Funnell, A. (2014, April 15). *The magic of technology, the technology of magic*. ABC Radio National. https://www.abc.net.au/radionational/programs/futuretense/5391382

Harry Houdini. (2019, January 31). *Harry Houdini*. Wikipedia. https://en.wikipedia.org/wiki/Harry_Houdini

James Randi. (2019, December 3). Wikipedia. https://en.wikipedia.org/wiki/James_Randi

Jean-Eugène Robert-Houdin. (2020, January 28). Wikipedia. https://en.wikipedia.org/wiki/Jean-Eug%C3%A8ne_Robert-Houdin

John Henry Anderson. (2022, January 25). Wikipedia. https://en.wikipedia.org/wiki/John_Henry_Anderson

John Nevil Maskelyne. (2022, January 17). Wikipedia. https://en.wikipedia.org/wiki/John_Nevil_Maskelyne

Lamont, P. (2015). Problems with the mapping of magic tricks. *Frontiers in Psychology*, *6*. https://doi.org/10.3389/fpsyg.2015.00855

LIFE Magazine. (1955, May 2). Old man's advice to youth: 'Never lose a holy curiosity. *LIFE Magazine*, 64.

Magic (illusion). (2022, February 1). Wikipedia. https://en.wikipedia.org/wiki/Magic_(illusion)#:~:text=Popular%2020th%2D%20and%2021st%2Dcentury

Penn & Teller. (2022, February 6). Wikipedia. https://en.wikipedia.org/wiki/Penn_%26_Teller

Pogue, D. (2017). Technology as magic. *Scientific American*, *317*(2), 26–26. https://doi.org/10.1038/scientificamerican0817-26

Quora. (2017). *What era can we take modern technology to that it would be regarded as magic?* Quora. https://www.quora.com/What-era-can-we-take-modern-technology-to-that-it-would-be-regarded-as-magic

Radcliffe-Brown, A. R. (1922). *The Andaman islanders: A study in social anthropology*. University Press.

Rensink, R. A., & Kuhn, G. (2015). The possibility of a science of magic. *Frontiers in Psychology*, *6*. https://doi.org/10.3389/fpsyg.2015.01576

Cover Image Sources (Public Domain): https://en.wikipedia.org/wiki/Harry_Houdini, https://en.wikipedia.org/wiki/David_Blaine, https://en.wikipedia.org/wiki/David_Copperfield_(illusionist)

AUTHOR RECOMMENDATIONS

Teach Yourself 25 Beginner Card Tricks!

Discover your inner magician, because this is one of the best basic card magic books on the market.

Get it now.

www.SFNonfictionBooks.com/Basic-Card-Magic

Teach Yourself 25 Easy Tricks with Everyday Objects!

Amaze your friends and family, because these magic tricks are easy to learn and fun to perform.

Get it now.

www.SFNonfictionBooks.com/Easy-Magic-Tricks

ABOUT SAM FURY

Sam Fury has had a passion for survival, evasion, resistance, and escape (SERE) training since he was a young boy growing up in Australia.

This led him to years of training and career experience in related subjects, including martial arts, military training, survival skills, outdoor sports, and sustainable living.

These days, Sam spends his time refining existing skills, gaining new skills, and sharing what he learns via the Survival Fitness Plan website.

www.SurvivalFitnessPlan.com

amazon.com/author/samfury

goodreads.com/SamFury

facebook.com/AuthorSamFury

instagram.com/AuthorSamFury

youtube.com/SurvivalFitnessPlan